PENGUIN BOOKS

a palace in the old village

TAHAR BEN JELLOUN was born in 1944 in Fez, Morocco, and immigrated to France in 1961. A novelist, essayist, critic, and poet, he is a regular contributor to *Le Monde*, *La Repubblica*, *El País*, and *Panorama*. His novels include *The Sacred Night* (winner of the 1987 Prix Goncourt), *Corruption*, *The Last Friend*, and *Leaving Tangier*. Ben Jelloun won the 1994 Prix Maghreb, and in 2004 he won the International IMPAC Dublin Literary Award for *This Blinding Absence of Light*.

LINDA COVERDALE has translated more than sixty books, including Tahar Ben Jelloun's award-winning novel *This Blinding Absence of Light*. A Chevalier de l'Ordre des Arts et des Lettres, she won the 2006 Scott Moncrieff Prize and the 1997 and 2008 French-American Foundation Translation Prize.

ALSO BY TAHAR BEN JELLOUN
PUBLISHED BY PENGUIN BOOKS

This Blinding Absence of Light
The Last Friend
Leaving Tangier

a palace in the old village

· a novel ·

TAHAR BEN JELLOUN

Translated from the French by
LINDA COVERDALE

PENGUIN BOOKS

PENGUIN BOOKS

Published by the Penguin Group

Penguin Group (USA) Inc., 375 Hudson Street, New York, New York 10014, U.S.A. · Penguin Group
(Canada), 90 Eglinton Avenue East, Suite 700, Toronto, Ontario, Canada M4P 2Y3 (a division of
Pearson Penguin Canada Inc.) · Penguin Books Ltd, 80 Strand, London WC2R 0RL, England ·
Penguin Ireland, 25 St Stephen's Green, Dublin 2, Ireland (a division of Penguin Books Ltd) · Penguin
Group (Australia), 250 Camberwell Road, Camberwell, Victoria 3124, Australia (a division of Pearson
Australia Group Pty Ltd) · Penguin Books India Pvt Ltd, 11 Community Centre, Panchsheel Park,
New Delhi – 110 017, India · Penguin Group (NZ), 67 Apollo Drive, Rosedale, North Shore 0632,
New Zealand (a division of Pearson New Zealand Ltd) · Penguin Books (South Africa) (Pty) Ltd,
24 Sturdee Avenue, Rosebank, Johannesburg 2196, South Africa

Penguin Books Ltd, Registered Offices:
80 Strand, London WC2R 0RL, England

First published in Penguin Books 2011

1 3 5 7 9 10 8 6 4 2

Originally published in French under the title *Au Pays* by Editions Gallimard, Paris.
This work is published with the support of the French Minister of Culture—
National Center of Books.
Ouvrage publié avec le concours du Ministère français chargé de la culture—Centre national du livre.

Publisher's Note
This is a work of fiction. Names, characters, places, and incidents either are the product of
the author's imagination or are used fictitiously, and any resemblance to actual persons,
living or dead, business establishments, events, or locales is entirely coincidental.

LIBRARY OF CONGRESS CATALOGING IN PUBLICATION DATA
Ben Jelloun, Tahar, 1944–
[Au pays. English]
A palace in the old village : a novel / Tahar Ben Jelloun ; translated from the French by
Linda Coverdale.
p. cm.
Originally published in French under the title: Au pays.
ISBN 978-0-14-311847-3
1. Moroccans—France—Fiction. 2. Immigrants—France—Fiction. 3. Home—Psychological
aspects—Fiction. 4. Parent and child—Fiction. 5. Conflict of generations—Fiction.
6. Morocco—Fiction. 7. Domestic fiction. 8. Psychological fiction. I. Coverdale, Linda.
II. Title.
PQ3989.2.J4A9413 2011
843'.914—dc22   2010043220

Printed in the United States of America
Set in Requiem · Designed by Elke Sigal

Translator's Note

The hero of this book passes "from one time to another, one life to another," changing "centuries, countries, customs." His disorientation is reflected in his misreading of the realities around him: there are things he cannot understand, and their importance completely escapes him. Since an American reader may well be similarly unfamiliar with some of the historical and cultural references in Ben Jelloun's novel, I have provided a few endnotes to explain these allusions, which are marked in the text by an asterisk.

a palace in the old village

I

When Mohammed had finished his evening prayer, he stayed sitting with his legs tucked beneath him on the small synthetic rug, gazing at a plastic made-in-China clock on the wall. He was looking, not at the hands, but at the picture surrounding the clock face: a crowd of people all in white, circling the Kaaba* beneath a blue sky thronged with birds and angels.

He was remembering his own pilgrimage, which had left him with mixed feelings. Although he'd been happy and deeply moved while praying, he'd been affected just as strongly by the oppressive lack of privacy and the rough way some pilgrims behaved. He could not understand why they were always shoving and stumbling into one another, occasionally even causing accidents that proved fatal.

He'd quickly learned that holy places disrupt ordinary perceptions. People are no longer themselves; they lose their bearings. Falling easily into trances, they lose consciousness as well, thus inviting a death much glorified in the ravings of charlatans. Such pilgrims die beneath the feet of stronger men, giants who trample others savagely, forging ahead without even a glance back to see what they've left in their wake, pressing on, their eyes and faces lifted heavenward as if such barbaric fervor had been demanded from on high. The weakest victims die, lying bloody in the dust. No eye falls upon them to offer a last prayer.

In holy places overrun within the space of a few days by more than two million Muslims—all intent on washing away their sins before returning home content, brimming with the virtues bestowed by their faith—these scenes were inevitable. It was not a pretty sight. Mohammed had always been afraid of crowds. In the grip of fanaticism, crowds become dangerous. It's best to avoid them, shun all confrontation, and escape being swept up in their momentum. At the factory, he would go on strike with his comrades but did not parade through the streets waving a sign.

Mohammed dreamed of a solitary springtime pilgrimage with only a few members of his tribe, just friends and family. Dreading violent situations, he was afraid of dying while in Mecca but was probably alone in his fear, for such a death sent one's soul straight to heaven. He never mentioned his dread of being crushed to death by fanatical feet, but he kept out of their way and studied them. What does such a foot look like?

It's dirty, sometimes bare, sometimes shod in a shabby *babouche*. Mohammed had encountered some of those wearers of dilapidated *babouches*. They were not from his country and spoke an Arab dialect he found impenetrable. Wherever did they come from? To Mohammed, a Muslim was an Arab or a Berber. He found it difficult to consider those other pilgrims Muslims. They were Africans, Chinese, Turks. All the pilgrims had fire in their eyes—the flame of faith, the passion of Islam. Why, he wondered, was his own gaze steady and serene? It was simply his temperament.

He had looked forward to that trip for a long time, had dreamed about it, even a bit too much, perhaps, just because he had no other grand projects in his life. He thought about his children's future, but this pained him, leaving him distressed and bewildered. So he performed his prayers and rituals in a strangely quiet way.

One morning, after emerging from the Great Mosque, he had not found his brand-new *babouches*, made by a craftsman in Fez. Astonished at having been robbed by another pilgrim, he could neither understand nor accept this. But he soon forgot his anger when one of the men who shared his room told him that every day, gangs attacked pilgrims to steal their money.

When a thief is captured, the man added, he gets his hand cut off. In fact, at the noon prayer today a few hands will be chopped off in public—you're invited to the show! A week ago they flogged a Yemeni for disrespecting the son of a prince, and last year they condemned a Christian to death—I think he was Italian—after they caught him with the daughter of an important Saudi family. A Muslim woman mustn't associate with—that is, be alone with—a non-Muslim, much less marry him. Oh no, they don't joke around here, they've got their laws: they claim they're in the Koran and they enforce them! We don't argue, us—we haven't the right. We come to meditate at the tomb of our beloved Prophet, we pray, we perform our rituals, and we go on home; that is, if we don't die trampled or missing a hand, because they can make mistakes and accuse you of stealing, and then your hand's gone in a flash, it's called swift justice, no time to think things over, and in any case, around here thinking is strongly discouraged, because here we give ourselves to God without any doubts or hesitation: we belong to God and God does what he wants with us. You got that, my friend?

Mohammed felt that lopping off a hand for stealing a slipper was too harsh, even cruel. He stared at his open hands for a long time and thought, Without them, I would have been nothing, not even a beggar. May Allah protect us from evil and misfortune!

A beggar held out his stump to him; Mohammed slipped some money into his pocket. He would have liked to talk with him, to learn his story. Perhaps he'd lost his hand in an accident or been the victim of some mistake—but the beggar had vanished.

Whenever Mohammed told people back home about his

pilgrimage, he got into trouble. Bachir, who had an opinion about everything, gave him a lecture between sips of a nice cool beer: A Muslim must not criticize what happens during the hajj. Leave that to the enemies of Islam, those who want to see us perpetually underdeveloped, in rags, dirty and inhuman. Now they've managed to label all Muslims terrorists! It's simple: we're doomed to stagnate or to slide backward, so criticism, forget about it, even if what you say is true—or else we'll stop calling you Hajji!

Mohammed had the last word, though, in his soft voice: If we don't criticize ourselves, we'll never get anywhere. Well, I'll keep quiet and wish you bon voyage, a good pilgrimage, but me, if I go back, it won't be during the main hajj. I'll choose the little one, the *umrah*. Besides, you know, we need to learn tolerance. For example: you drink, but I never mention it, that's your business and I'm not going to scold you—so stop criticizing those who have the courage to criticize themselves!

A big buzzing fly roused Mohammed from his reverie and kept blindly bumping into the wall. He would have liked to rescue it but hadn't the energy. The fly went around and around in that room as if it too were a prisoner. Mohammed bowed his head. He seemed to be answering a call, listening to a voice—a sort of whisper escaping from a crack in the plaster, a fissure the wallpaper from the sixties could no longer seal up. The apartment building was in such disrepair that both the municipality and the public housing authority had dropped it from their rolls; it needed too much work, especially since the chaotic arrival of huge numbers of new African immigrants.

Those from the Maghreb—Morocco, Algeria, Tunisia—formed a volatile mix with the black Africans, sparking racist insults and fights between adolescents from both sides. Mohammed no longer knew whether this racism sprang primarily from the color of their skin or from extreme poverty. He found himself remembering an old uncle with business dealings in black Africa who'd brought home to Morocco a Senegalese woman whom the whole village had considered a slave, a nonperson. Mohammed had been a child at the time, but he was still haunted by what had happened: the African woman, who spoke neither Arabic nor Berber, was driven from the village after his uncle went abroad again to work. The entire community banded against her because she was black and they couldn't understand a word she said. She fled on foot, and that was the last they saw of her.

This woman, whom no one ever spoke of again, still wandered among Mohammed's childhood memories. Where was she now? Had she died? Gone home? He had no idea, and wound up thinking that the woman was eternal: she would never die. This one memory had convinced him—and to Mohammed this was obvious—that skin color and poverty ganged up easily to reject a human being whose sole crime was not being white and rich. Racism horrified him. The first time he'd heard someone called a raghead was in a train where a conductor was yelling at an elderly Algerian man who couldn't find his ticket. Without knowing what the word meant, Mohammed could tell it was insulting, unkind. The Algerian had stood up and begun taking off his clothes as if he were going to be frisked. All right, all right, the conductor had grumbled. These ragheads never understand anything!

Mohammed would have loved to move out of his apartment building in the projects, but that would create other problems and mean living farther away from his children, so he put up with his daily hell and tried to keep his kids from succumbing to racism. You have to understand, he told them, these Africans may be quite different from us—they're poorer, there are more of them—but they aren't bad people, so be tolerant.

Poverty, insecurity, and overcrowding left no room for dialogue or tolerance, however. People felt helpless and completely fed up. There wasn't a single French family left in the building. All who could leave had fled, and the police simply let the projects stew in their own juice.

Mohammed had always dreamed of a house, a big, beautiful house where his whole family could be together in happiness, harmony, and mutual respect. A house nestled among trees and gardens, awash in light and color, an open, peaceful

house where not only would everyone feel content but all conflicts and difficulties would be resolved as if by magic. It would
be a little bit of paradise amid the soft rustle of trees and the
murmuring of water. A stubborn dream, but he knew that one
day he would make it come true. He never spoke of it to anyone, not even his wife, who would have taken him for a gentle
madman, off in his own world with his head in the clouds.
Mohammed kept his thoughts and fantasies to himself. He
wasn't much of a talker. At the dinner table, he'd complain
about rising prices and a salary that wasn't enough anymore:
Before—a long time ago—I was able to save money, but now I
don't understand how it can go so quickly. Then he'd fall silent.

Alone on his prayer rug, Mohammed mumbled a few more
short verses from the Koran. Then he began to sense something
holding him fast, preventing him from standing up. He felt
heavy, as if he had a weight on his back. He tried to move but
couldn't manage to stretch out his legs. He bowed his head
again and immediately felt overcome by a slight drowsiness.
The fly killed itself, all on its own, drowning in a glass of tea.
What an idiot, Mohammed thought.

The wall was talking to him. He leaned forward: that same
voice again, speaking to him in his dialect. He relaxed. He
opened the Koran and pretended to immerse himself in it. Even
though he couldn't read it, he loved the company of this book.

He loved its calligraphy, its binding of green leatherette, the whole aura of its importance. It was the only book he'd taken with him on the day he'd left Morocco. It was wrapped in a piece of white cloth that had been cut, following tradition, from his father's shroud. This book was everything to Mohammed: his culture, his identity, his passport, his pride, his secret. He opened it delicately, pressed it to his heart, brought it to his lips, and gently kissed it. He believed that everything was there. Those who can read find within it all the wisdom of the world, all its explanations.

Not only did Mohammed sincerely believe this, but an *alem*, a Muslim sage, the imam of the main mosque in the *département* of Yvelines, had absolutely confirmed it: Allah created the universe; he sent his messengers to speak to men and women; he knows what each of us is thinking; he even knows what we don't know, what is buried within us, so you see, the Koran is the key to all Creation. It is no accident that more and more people throughout the world are embracing Islam! Our numbers are constantly growing, and that's what frightens America and its friends, you know: we have a treasure, and this upsets them. They want to see Muslims wallowing in destitution or with bombs strapped to our waists, so that's Islam to them—poverty or a bomb! They're envious of our religion's success around the globe! You heard about that dog who drew our prophet—may the blessing of God be upon him!—with a turban stuffed with bombs? Can you believe that? They're just provoking us: they want to humiliate us, make fun of us, but God is waiting for them, and they will crawl on their bellies before him, begging for mercy, terrified of spending all eternity in hell, for God is great, and his word is the only truth!

Mohammed would have liked to reply but hadn't the courage to tell the imam, for example, that it was imbeciles like him who praise jihad, babbling of paradise and martyrdom, yes, retards like him who send floundering young men who can't find their own way in life off to die, because liars and hypocrites like him push youngsters into the arms of death, saying: You'll be real martyrs, as true and good as the ones in the days of the Prophet, and you'll be buried in clothes soaked in the blood of sacrifice, not in the shroud of an ordinary death! You will go straight to God, who awaits you in paradise! Make your ablutions in preparation, for it is better to enter the house of God cleansed in readiness for eternal prayer.

Mohammed had heard about that business with the cartoons, but he'd paid no attention. He was profoundly convinced that the Prophet was a spirit, not a face that could be drawn. It was only common sense. As usual, he kept his thoughts to himself. There was nothing to see in Mohammed's face except immense sadness, a kind of pernicious resignation he could not throw off. He would have liked to lose himself in reading, to discuss different interpretations of the Koran, but he knew he was condemned to the ignorance that had stuck to him since childhood. His heart's delight was to see his children doing their homework at the dining-room table just before dinner. He watched them with love and a touch of envy. He adored going with them to the stationery section of the supermarket to buy their school supplies and never missed this yearly ritual that so excited them. He would take the day off to satisfy all their requests. At home he helped them put covers on their notebooks and textbooks. He had put up shelves to hold their books, which he often tidied up and kept dusted for them.

He may not have known how to read the Koran, but he knew that Allah condemns hypocrites and murderers. He had learned the book by heart, like all country children. He recited it mechanically, made the occasional mistake, told God he was sorry, and started over again at the beginning of the sura,* plunging on all the way to the end, for any hesitation or interruption would make him lose his place. Only the imam of Yvelines was able to quote a verse and pause to provide commentary.

The imam had memorized the book, which he claimed to have studied in Cairo, at the venerable university of al-Azhar. Perhaps this was true; there was no way to challenge him. No one had seen this imam arrive. He had appeared out of the blue and surrounded himself with an entourage of young delinquents determined to go straight. He called them "my children." He had a big car, wore lovely white robes, scented himself with sandalwood oil, and did not live in Mohammed's slum neighborhood. Rumor assigned him two wives along with between ten and a dozen offspring. He addressed people in classical Arabic and sometimes in French, which he mangled. Moroccans looked at one another and wondered: Just who does he think we are? Where did he come from? Who's paying him? People figured he must be receiving money from wealthy countries.

They suspected that he was an Egyptian hired by the Saudis. Moroccans distrusted people from the Gulf States, who for years had come to their country, especially to Tangier, to hole up in hotels and send out for girls and booze. Mohammed had often heard about that. He had never seen these people in white robes, but many nasty things were said about those who came to Morocco to indulge their vices. Extraordinary rumors sometimes circulated, about outlandish orgies. It seems a minister once lent his pretty wife to a powerful emir from Kuwait or Dubai, and she came home missing a breast! The fellow had bitten, and then eaten, her breast. No one, of course, had seen that one-breasted woman; no one had proof of anything whatsoever, but as they say, "Where there's smoke . . ." A cannibal Kuwaiti! That's how the citizens of the Gulf figured in the popular imagination—men who suckle at the breasts of beautiful women and on occasion go even further.

There was another unbelievable story that made the rounds

of the cafés: to gain entrance to the women's section of a hammam, or Turkish bath, the cousin of an emir's chauffeur had disguised himself as a woman and, when discovered, had been beaten by the ladies—who'd poured buckets of boiling water on his genitals. The man had run outside screaming, his balls in a pitiful state. But so many, many stories were told about these people that the government had finally intervened to put an end to such crude rumors.

Mohammed had been staring at the wall for so long that he began to think he was drawing closer to it or, rather, that the wall was advancing toward him. He felt trapped in that little room, which his children never entered. He had the impression that the voice was talking to him about his retirement. That word, "retirement," flitted through the air just like that big buzzing fly.

Mohammed's mind was elsewhere, however, in Mecca or the mosque of his childhood. His thoughts had turned toward the village, back to a colorless time of strange solitude. Because of lice, scabies, and other afflictions, the butcher, who doubled as a barber, had shaved all the children's heads, and whenever Mohammed had rubbed his hand over his scalp, he'd felt a kind of boil, slightly infected. Those days had the acrid smell of Fly-Tox and antilouse powder, but there was also the taste of pure honey and argan oil. He well remembered the meals his girl cousin would bring to him after he'd taken out the livestock: heavily sugared mint tea, crêpes, honey, oil, and occasionally a bit of *amlou*, an almond paste mixed with argan oil, honey, and a few spices. The mornings were cool and quiet. In the natural course of things, his cousin would become his wife, but they almost never spoke when together. They would look at each other; she would lower her eyes, then leave.

One day her little brother brought the food, and Mohammed understood that the time for the marriage proposal had arrived. His cousin was quite young, barely fifteen, yet the next summer would see them married. Sweet memories, full of tenderness, modesty, and peace. Mohammed loved the silences that could last the entire morning, and would let himself sink into reverie.

For the marriage ceremony, the best singer in the area had come with his *cheíkhats* and musicians. They had sung and danced until dawn. Vulgar, professional, and efficient, the *cheíkhats* were female singers who looked like gypsies and stank of clove oil. As the ceremonial prince, Mohammed led his wife to the house of his parents, who had discreetly absented themselves to allow the newlyweds to be alone. Once more silence fell like a brief night on the young couple, who did not say a word to each other. That was the tradition. Mohammed said his prayer and pinched out the candle. It all happened in the dark. He'd been very intimidated and, above all, inexperienced. For him as for her, it was clearly the first time. He let himself be guided by instinct, and the blood traced a pretty design on the sheet. Honor was saved. After a few days of celebration, the village returned to its routine.

Mohammed had already been thinking about joining his uncle, who had emigrated to northern France, and for that he needed a passport, the little green booklet with the star of Morocco stamped in the center of its cover. At the time, such documents were granted only to well-off city families. Every now and then the *caïd*, the local headman, would receive orders from Rabat: Need 104 robust men in good health for France. The *caïd* would arrive in the village in a jeep driven by the state police, an arrival heralded from afar by billowing dust. Taking himself very seriously, the *caïd* would first require some refreshments, then have the village men pass before him in review. The *caïd* scrupulously imitated everything the French had done during their colonial occupation, and despite being barely able to read he kept a dossier at hand, which he would leaf through from time to time. França is waiting for you. Do not shame us. Be men, soldiers, worthy representatives of our country! The jeep would drive off, leaving behind its cloud of ocher dust and a few wives in tears.

2

The voice was insistent and was now addressing Moham-med in French, a language he had finally learned to understand but did not use. It was only thanks to his children that he knew a few words of it, because they would speak nothing but French to him, which made him deeply unhappy. He had patiently taught them a few elements of Berber, but for nothing: they persisted in speaking French and made fun of him when he mispronounced it.

And now this unknown voice was talking to him in that tongue, repeating a word he knew perfectly but did not want to discuss. That's what it was: a word he did not want to hear, a word echoing like a condemnation, announcing the fateful date he wanted to postpone until later—as late as possible. It wasn't death, but something very similar, and it had nothing to do with Mecca. He had so dreaded this day, this moment. It wasn't a question of a trip, a holiday, or a long and lovely stroll around Medina at a time outside the official period of pilgrimage, no—the voice was telling him something specific, definitive, and irreversible: to stop working. To break a rhythm acquired over forty years, to change his habits, to no longer rise at 5:00 A.M. and put on his gray overalls, to adapt to a new life, turn over a new leaf, change his mind, toss away the crutches of his old routines, those familiar landmarks. To stop working was to learn to be politely bored and do nothing, while trying not to sink into melancholy. Work didn't make him happy, perhaps, but it kept him occupied, kept him from thinking.

Mohammed was afraid. Afraid of having to climb mountains, pyramids of stones. Afraid of tumbling into the ravine of the absurd, of having to face each of his children, over whom he had lost every scrap of authority. Afraid of accepting a life in which he no longer controlled much of anything. He lived *through his routine*, the long straight line that carried on regardless. He'd gotten used to this and didn't want to change, didn't want anything else. Everything seemed difficult to him, complicated, and he knew he was not made for conflicts, for combat. He had never fought; even as a child he'd stayed on the sidelines, watching others get into fights, then slipping away, wondering why there was such violence in a place so far from the city and forgotten by God. Working kept thoughts like that at a distance.

At night he counted on his physical fatigue to put him to

sleep before he had to confront the familiar mountain, which kept growing bigger. Sometimes it came to him wreathed in thunderclaps, then toppled onto his back and buried him. He would see heavy stones piling up on his body, crushing the breath from him as he lay paralyzed and defenseless. He wasn't in pain but in trouble, pinned down. When the mountain finally withdrew, leaving him for dead, he would wake up, drink a large glass of water, and go sit in the kitchen to wait for dawn. To keep busy, sometimes he cleaned the spotless floor—old linoleum printed to look like wood—by polishing it with a wet rag. He'd rearrange the small stock of provisions, check the refrigerator to make a mental note of what was needed, brew himself some tea, and study the sky while awaiting the first gleam of sunrise.

He'd never thought the ax would fall so soon, so brutally. He was stunned. Lost. And already in mourning, because there was no escape from retirement, or, as he called it, "'tirement." No matter how often his children corrected him, he still said "'tirement." That was his invisible, two-faced enemy, because even though for some people it represented freedom, to him it meant the end of life. Period. The end of everything. No more daily routine, no more paid vacations back home, year after year. Well-earned vacations! His conscience was clear: he had worked hard to earn his living. He detested easy money, hated cheaters, swindlers, loathed fraud and deceit. He'd seen how some of his coworkers' children lived; he knew what "fell off a truck" meant and had expressly forbidden his children to buy stolen goods.

On the first day in July, he would fill the family car with suitcases and gifts and head straight down the road, like a migratory bird anxious to catch up with the flock. He didn't speed, rarely stopped, and was happy only when he reached his village, a full 2,882 kilometers from Yvelines. The children and their mother would sleep; he alone drove on and on, covering the distance with impeccably steady resolve. Sometimes he drove with another family—the cars would take turns following each other—but he really preferred to make the trip as the sole person in charge. At the wheel he had but one thought: to get to his house in the village, arrive at the best time to hand out the presents, visit his parents' tomb the next day, go to the hammam, get a massage from Massoud, and eat crêpes prepared by his elderly aunt. He drove, and in his mind's eye he saw all that in living color, bathed in light. He used to smile to himself while his wife slept beside him in the front seat.

At the automobile plant, Mohammed was a creature of habit. Always on time. Determined never to be late or absent. Except when bedridden with flu, he insisted on going to work even if he was sick. He brought his lunch, ate quickly, parked himself on a bench, and closed his eyes. When his comrades teased him, he replied that he needed this little doze, a ritual that never took more than ten minutes. He was as reliable as an expensive watch. Never angry, never at fault: a model worker. In fact, he dreaded the thought of botching anything, being reprimanded; he couldn't have handled that. At first he was assigned to the automotive assembly line, moving later to the painting shop, which was less tiring but more dangerous. He worked there with a face mask. His health hadn't suffered; he didn't smoke, had never touched alcohol. He had a sound body, which too much sugary mint tea was threatening with the first signs of diabetes.

Retirement? No, not for him—and especially not now! What was it, anyway? Who invented it? It was as if they were telling him he was sick and no longer useful to society. An incurable illness, a prognosis of endless ennui—that's what it was, a curse, although he knew other workers longed for it impatiently. Well, he didn't. He didn't think about it. He'd watched his pals retire, and the next thing he knew, death had done for them. Retirement was the introduction to death, lurking at the end of the tunnel. It was a trap, a diabolical invention. He saw no need for it and no possible benefits, especially to his health. No, he was convinced that the real face of retirement was just a skull wearing makeup.

The memory of Brahim then flared up like a flame in the darkness: Brahim, who died five months after leaving the plant in good health, permanently retired by 'tirement. Yes, done in by utter uselessness, condemned to die a few months after his sixtieth birthday. Sentenced by silence to die of idle loneliness. He, Mohammed, was useful! Whenever flu laid him low, knocked him clean off his feet, he knew the assembly line would be less productive, less profitable that day. One morning when his car broke down, he'd raised the hood to see what was wrong and thought, This is a flu car! Whenever he was out sick, nuts, bolts, and other things did not get properly tightened and adjusted. Mohammed was so strict, so meticulous at his job, that he figured the car company would soon collapse if it put him out to pasture. Being useful was vital to him, in fact he wondered how the factory could survive without him, without his obsessively conscientious care, and without men like Brahim, or Habib, who'd quit overnight after winning 752,302 francs in the lottery. Then Mohammed remembered Brahim's only daughter, who had married a Senegalese and abandoned her family. That story had made the rounds of every Maghrebian family in Yvelines and beyond.

Kader and his spiteful tongue had had a field day, unleashing all his hatred for black Africans: Brahim gave his girl to a black! A black went off with his only daughter! Blacks and Arabs can't mix! Berbers and blacks aren't meant to marry. We're not racist, but the tribe has to stick together! Our daughters should stay within the tribe. At least if he'd been Algerian or Tunisian, there'd be less talk! Back in Morocco, we call blacks *abid*, "slaves," and we don't mix. That girl must be a natural-born slut, you know what I mean? Racist we're not, but to each his own! Me, I've nothing against black Africans, I even think they're okay, but what I can't stand, it's their smell, and yes, we *all* have a smell, but me, I'm allergic to the smell of Africans, I can't help it, but I'm not racist, and besides, they probably can't stand our smell, either. Brahim should have laid down the law—there's no way his daughter would have disobeyed him!

But Kader, you *know* we have no control over our children now, and for the slightest thing, a little slap, a light tap on the shoulder, they up and call the police! It's LaFrance keeping us from educating our children, LaFrance giving them too many rights, and then it's us in the shit. France, Belgium, Holland— those countries haven't a clue what authority is anymore.

Too true, my brother, children here are not like those back home: here you can't raise your hand or chastise them for coming home late or not doing their homework—here everything is ass backward! Poor Brahim, he hasn't slept a wink since that business. His wife left him; he's just a shadow of himself, victimized by his daughter, gone off to make babies with a black who claims to work in a bank when the truth of it is, he's a doorman there, so not only do they smell, they lie! We Algerians, we have no blacks at home, while you Moroccans and Tunisians, you've got plenty of them, 'specially in the southern provinces, so if Brahim's daughter plays "knees up" with a Negro, it's because where you come from other women do it too!

Well, you, you're just looking for a fight. Algerians are all aggressive, they're violent and don't like the other countries of the Maghreb, everyone knows that, so if Brahim gave his daughter to an African, it proves that us, *we're* not racists!

Pondering that episode, Mohammed had to admit that although immigrants from the Maghreb were the targets of racism in Europe, they in turn despised black Africans, whether in France or at home in their own countries. Racism is everywhere! he thought. How would he have reacted if one of his girls had married an African? He even found it hard to imagine such a situation until he sorted things out by considering Moha Touré, his coworker from Mali on the assembly line. He knew Moha's family well and had been impressed by the education this man had managed to give his children. I'd rather my daughter married one of Moha's sons, he told himself, than a Christian boy who hasn't even been circumcised. Moha was an observant Muslim, unprejudiced, and especially concerned with presenting a good image of Islam. He lectured his children—taught them manners, tolerance, and respect. He was lucky, because they obeyed him. Mohammed's kids did whatever they wanted. He had no say.

3

Mohammed thought about his five children. They would stand by him, no question; they wouldn't abandon him or let him fall prey to sadness but take care of him, fuss over him, give him presents, send him on another pilgrimage to Mecca. No, the children were his pride and his protection against feeling lonesome. They respected him even though they rarely spoke with him. He never said much to them, either; they hadn't a great deal to talk about. When a problem arose, they'd go to their mother, who would then talk it over with him. Habit and tradition.

They hadn't seen a lot of their father. He'd always left for the automobile plant while they were asleep, come home in the afternoon, and gone to his room to rest. He praised them when they received good grades at school. He gazed at them tenderly and gave them big smiles. On Sundays he saw his pals at the mosque, then at the Café Hassan, which served no alcohol. It was a place of weary melancholy. Strictly male clientele, some of whom played dominoes. Against the background of a TV always tuned to a Moroccan station, they discussed the high cost of real estate in Agadir and Marrakech or watched Parliament in session and ridiculed those Westernized men dressed up in white djellabas. They talked about plans to go home and sometimes discussed their thorniest problem: their children's future.

So all that only to wind up without our children! No, that's not quite it. Let's just say that our kids are more up-to-the-minute than we are. They've discovered modern life and they love it. When you take them home to the countryside, they find everything old-fashioned, don't like it; at first they're happy enough, but then they get bored, they're tourists, tourists in their own country, but they're not even curious about it, they're uncomfortable and don't understand why we love being there while they complain about the dust, the flies, the starving cats, and the old people who do nothing. The landscapes seem weird to them; they expect to see some hero from *Star Wars* pop up with a light sword in his hand. They wait for something to happen. Nothing, absolutely nothing happens. There are only stones, prickly pear cacti, and dogs staggering around in the stifling heat. Back home is the back of beyond: tons of boredom. It's hard to talk to our children about our roots. They've no idea what home means to us!

But just a minute, my brother! It isn't their country, let me explain this to you: it's *your* country, you're the one who's attached to it, while they see it through the eyes of foreigners, and most of them don't even speak the language, so the truth of it is, it's our fault, for not teaching them Arabic or Berber! I'm not going back, that's for sure. When I get my 'tirement, I'm setting myself up here, I'll open a small café and wait for them to give me some grandchildren! I sold the house in Agadir, at a good price. It was French retirees who bought it; they're going to live out their lives over there, in the sun—it's the world turned upside down! And look at the Frenchies themselves: they have kids, who then leave them behind to fend for themselves, and they all go their own ways!

Yes, you're right, the parents do the best they can, and then one day it's real hot, really, *really* hot; it's a huge heat wave, and then they croak, alone: fifteen thousand old people died from the heat, can you imagine? Alone, with nobody to give them a glass of water, and where were the children? On vacation. Hey, wait a minute—lots of them were in Agadir for the sun and the sea, while their parents were dying alone back in France like animals forgotten by the roadside!* Well, if my son does that to me, I'll . . . kill him—no, I'll disown him—but our children are blessed, they won't let us die like dogs!

It's true: in Morocco we don't have old folks' homes. We're not modern, but we've still got some good things going for us. You know, the children of the people killed by the heat, they didn't all come home to bury them. Some of them waited for LaFrance to do that before they bothered to show up! Why? I don't understand! It was just because. Because they didn't want to pay for the funerals. Oh yes, my friend, they pinch every sou in this country, they're not like us. Our parents—Allah said you owe them respect or you'll go to hell.

Allah says lots of things. He even says it's our mothers who get us into paradise!

Allah said that? I don't remember it.

Well, then you're a godless fool!

Mohammed recalled the story of the man everyone called Momo, Hajji Momo, tall and thin, always wearing a greasy old cap of threadbare velvet, a former soldier in the French army who had left his village in the Aurès Mountains of eastern Algeria to make war against the Germans, to liberate France. He'd had a fight with his brothers and sisters about an inheritance and had been so disgusted that he never again wanted anything to do with that family tearing itself apart over money. He'd gone off to war, fought like a lion, and then in 1945, instead of going back home, decided to stay in France. There he met Martine, a buxom and warm-hearted woman from Normandy. His military pension was not enough to live on, so he worked for Renault with the same energy he'd shown during the war. He was a good man, but he had one fault: he drank. He sobered up in Mecca and for three months did not touch a drop of alcohol. When he returned, however, Martine went through a depression—Momo never knew why—and left him. Momo went straight back into alcoholic hell. Abandoned, without children, he died alone in their tiny apartment and was found three days later. The Arab community was stunned: this was the first time an immigrant had died utterly alone, as sometimes happens in French society. Dying so forlorn, that was intolerable. People had thought this would never happen to Muslims because they all belonged to the same clan, the same house, the house of Islam, which unites the rich and the poor, the great and the humble.

The shadows of Brahim and Momo haunted Mohammed's thoughts. The life left in front of him, he reasoned, was bound to be shorter than the life behind him. It wasn't death that frightened him; it was what led up to and brought on death that preoccupied him, even though he was counting on his faith for comfort. That left loneliness, which didn't scare him, because he was absolutely sure that neither his wife nor his children would abandon him. But the specter of solitude kept him constant company anyway.

It was during this period of doubt that Mohammed ran away. Like an angry adolescent, he decided one day not to go home as usual after work. He took a different train and wound up where he'd never been before. It was in late spring, when the air was mild; the landscapes had pretty colors, passersby were smiling, and some said hello to him. He felt buoyant, imbued with the energy of his childhood. Fewer people from the Maghreb lived there; it was mostly eastern Europeans. He went into a bar and asked for a nonalcoholic beer. The waiter, who had his back turned, replied, We don't carry that stuff here! Thinking he'd made a gaffe, Mohammed ordered a Coke. Still busily cleaning glasses, the waiter said without turning around, With ice, lemon, or nothing? Nothing. The man slid a can of Coke down the bar to Mohammed, who would have liked a straw but didn't dare ask for one. Making an effort, he said softly, Omelet, I'd like an omelet. The waiter came over, looked him in the face, and shouted, An omelet how? Your choices are country ham and cheese, Parisian ham and button mushrooms, Spanish ham and cheese, Italian prosciutto. . . . I'd like just an omelet, with nothing else. I don't eat pork. . . . Ah! You're a Muslim! But with a plain omelet, a little glass of white would go very nicely! No, I don't drink alcohol either. So it'll be a plain omelet! Not even *aux fines herbes*? Plain, yes, just eggs and a bit of butter.

He'd rarely eaten an omelet as good as that one. It was nothing special, but he had done something out of the ordinary, so everything seemed wonderful to him. He told himself he ought to have this sort of escapade again.

And yet, as he left the bar he felt strange. He was having trouble digesting the eggs and all that butter. He thought about his wife, who was probably starting to worry; he could have phoned but didn't know what to say to her. He was incapable of lying, of coming up with credible scenarios. He would have been ashamed to admit he'd taken off like that because he'd felt dejected and wanted to play a trick on his routine.

He took the train back in the other direction, reaching his neighborhood forty minutes later. It was evening. Families were watching television. A few young people were hanging around here and there. One called out to him: Hey, Pops, you in the market for the real thing, some good homegrown? If you don't use, at least give some to your kids! Just joking, you old fart!

Old fart! He'd heard that insult many times before, but never directed at him. As he walked home, head hanging, he wondered if he really looked like an old fart. What is an old fart? Must be a pathetic guy, someone who doesn't fight back, who endures life, and the day he decides not to go through the same motions, he runs into a fresh kind of hostility. He has never found where he belongs. Outside of the painting shop at the plant, he's in the way, he feels unwanted, and at home the routine is even more painful because of occasional small scenes with the children. Perhaps he'd rather have lived at the plant, where he was needed, where the assembly line depended on him for its smooth operation. He'd noticed behind the foreman's desk a little corner that he'd have really liked to make his own, his home, his bed, his refuge, but he would have missed the children, even if he was beginning to get the idea that they didn't miss him much; in any case, they kept their feelings hidden. They'd become little Europeans, looking out for themselves, pushing their parents into the background.

The guy who murdered his wife and three children but botched his own death—he must be "an old fart." There'd been a lot about him on TV. To kill and then attempt suicide because of debts or regret over a wasted life, that was something Mohammed did not understand. Suicide was forbidden in Islam. And anyone who commits suicide is punished by God for all eternity, forced to repeat his action forever. Just imagine a guy who hangs himself: until the end of time he'll be hanging himself, maybe not from the same tree but in houses, stores, right in the middle of a wealthy family's living room. . . .

Mohammed suddenly thought, Wait: will there be houses and stores in the afterlife? I know, no one has ever returned to tell us what goes on there. Kill? That's horrible, I'd never do that! At the celebration of Eid al-Kebir, I used to refuse to cut the sheep's throat, leaving that to my older brother or our neighbor. The sight of blood upsets me. I've never raised my hand to my children, always tried to restrain my temper. At the same time, I've indulged them too much, especially my youngest girl—so spoiled she became a terrible student. I realized this when she decided to drop out of high school. That day, I cried all alone after prayers. To me, it was more than a failure, a humiliation. I don't like school, she told me, I'm quitting, and anyway I want to get a job. I understood then that any attempt to set her straight would be useless. I could have told her, If you only knew how I suffered from not getting to attend school, from missing out on so many things because I'm illiterate. If you had any idea what I'd give today to have knowledge, expertise, education, diplomas, but I feel like a donkey, a faithful animal going along the same road every day, doing the same things, unable to vary my routine for fear I'll get lost, afraid of drowning in a calm sea. Oh, if you knew how alone I feel because I need someone to help me whenever I go into an administrative office, but all that, I guess it has nothing to do with you, you were born in a different time, you found life a little easier, a little less puzzling.

You children don't like to be reminded of what we others have gone through. Remember the day when you wiped your knife on a piece of bread? I had a fit: bread isn't a scrap of rag! I was taught to bring bread to my lips and kiss it before taking a bite or putting it away. Bread is sacred, and you, you were treating it as a thing of no importance. You didn't understand my reaction, especially since you weren't used to seeing me react at all. Then there was that time you turned up your nose at some bananas, pushing them away with your fingertips and saying, Don't like them. I made the mistake of saying that when I was your age I dreamed of eating bananas and apples, and that I'd had to wait till I came to France to taste them. But that didn't interest you or your brothers and sisters. It's like the time your brother Mourad talked back to me when I was objecting to the people he was friends with, when he said, I hope I don't turn out like you, oh no, not like you: you're there and no one sees you, so excuse me, but you don't make me want to be like you at all.

I looked at myself in the mirror for a long time, but I never figured out why my son wouldn't want to be like me. What's so crummy, so repulsive about me? I'm clean, I don't hurt anyone, I do my work the best I can, I'm faithful to God and carry out my duties, and none of that shows in my face! Maybe I should turn mean, wasting the family money in bars with whores, dragging around in the streets like Atiq, that guy who lost everything, especially his mind.

Except for the youngest daughter, Rekya, each of his children had had a different reason for going away, and Mohammed's house had slowly emptied out. Mohammed had a hard time coming to grips with this. He hadn't noticed that they were growing up, choosing their paths, then leaving on them. Angry at himself for not having paid more attention, he took comfort in the fact that other parents were in the same boat. Then he brooded over the evil influence of a charlatan he held responsible for his empty nest, one of those old Berbers who take up sorcery, fortune-telling, and other services to plump up their bank accounts for their old age. These con artists let their beards grow, dress in traditional clothing, set themselves up in a small apartment, surround themselves with books on Islam, and burn a bit of incense. They hang calligraphed names of Allah and his prophet Mohammed on the wall next to photos of Mecca and Medina; on the floor lie prayer rugs with the image of the Kaaba. They claim to do no evil, simply to protect people from it. As a good Muslim, Mohammed detested such sorcerers. His wife and even his eldest daughter, Jamila, consulted a certain Allam, who extracted tidy sums from them in exchange for talismans to carry or hide among their belongings.

One day Jamila had been pulled aside by security agents at Orly Airport: in her purse, wrapped in tinfoil and duct tape, was a small unidentified object that the agents suspected was drugs or an ingredient for a bomb. They had active imaginations. Jamila had opened the wad to reveal a strip of brown fabric on which Allam had scribbled in Arabic a protective talisman that had unfortunately proved powerless to deflect the attention of the security staff. During the flight, his daughter had reflected on how ridiculous it was for a modern young woman like her, born in Yvelines, to be carrying in her purse— along with (among other things) a cell phone, a bottle of perfume, some lipstick, and a PDA—a scrap of dirty material for her mental and physical safety! But a little later, when the plane encountered some frightening turbulence, Jamila couldn't help halfway blaming the storm on the fact that the talisman had been opened and incorrectly closed. I was sure born in France, she concluded, but my genes come from the old country!

What could Mohammed do? His entire village practiced this kind of magic. His wife occasionally burned herbs with a suffocating smell and asked him to stand in the smoke for seven minutes. Because he avoided conflict, he did as she asked instead of arguing; he had no choice if he wanted peace in his home. He walked around and around the little brazier so the nauseating herbal odors could affect the course of his life. His wife was a good woman, though; illiterate perhaps but intelligent, courageous, and thrifty. She never became angry, patiently put up with her children's behavior, and served her husband without grumbling, of course: protest was useless. She'd seen what had happened to Lubna, a young village woman who married too young and was taken to France by her husband. Lubna had tried to rebel, refusing to cook and clean the house, but her husband had boxed her ears so hard that she'd been deaf for a good hour. When she went to the police, the husband denied everything, then sent her back to the village as a repudiated wife. He'd written ahead to ask her father to take away her passport and throw it in the fire.

———————

Mohammed preferred the Book. He liked things to be simple and obvious. He was fond of the olive oil and pure honey his elderly uncle brought him. Although Mohammed was diabetic, his uncle had persuaded him that pure honey was completely compatible with diabetes: You can eat as much of this as you want; honey is wonderful for the health. What you should avoid is white sugar, city sugar. Honey can only do you good! Allah talks about it in the Koran: there will be exquisite honey in paradise, rivers of honey—it can't be bad for you. So Mohammed ate some every morning before going to the plant. His diabetes was getting worse, drying his mouth, but he would not give up his honey. Hot bread soaked in olive oil then dipped in a bowl of honey—that was his treat, his pleasure.

Mohammed took medications, and his wife had given him a talisman tightly sewn up in a scrap of gray cloth, probably the same kind his daughter carried. It will protect you against illness, the evil eye, and even against the heat in the plant! He pretended to believe her; he didn't want to give up his morning feast. As for the Book, enveloped in a swatch of the paternal shroud, every day he slipped it inside a plastic bag bearing the logo of a local supermarket. Whenever he opened the book and brought it to his lips, he was no longer alone. No need for the services of al-Hajj, the sorcerer of the Porte de la Chapelle neighborhood in Paris; no, he refused to go see him, and although Mohammed carried the man's talismans around with him, that was because he didn't want to hurt his wife's feelings.

Avoiding arguments with his wife or colleagues was a priority, and he found disputes over material things particularly pointless. He minded his business, quietly, inoffensively. When there was a strike, he went along with everyone else, never took the lead, followed Marcel's orders, waited for the whole thing to blow over. It's not my problem, he said. The French are used to going on strike, so I do as they do, and sometimes I don't even know why we've stopped work, so Marcel explains it to me, and while I'm listening I think about something else, like my childhood back home, and I smile, because if I'd stayed home no French fellow would ever have taken the trouble to tell me the reasons for a strike, political or whatever, and no European would have asked for my opinion! It's really your decision, Marcel tells me. You can vote against the strike, that's your right; we've got a democracy here.

The first time Mohammed had heard that word was in a café in Marrakech, one day while he was waiting for the bus to Tangier. Someone on the radio was shouting, "Demokratia al hakikya!" Democracy and truth. Later, on the bus, a man sat down next to him and began explaining what it was all about: You see, we who live out in the country, when we go to the city we feel like we don't belong, but with *demokratia* we'll get better treatment—that's what a guy said on the radio the other day, that we'll all be equal and our children will go to public school for free, like hospitals and medicines will be too, but to get that you have to go vote, even if you can't read, so you just put your fingerprints in a notebook, then you vote, that's *demokratía*, and then we'll get water, electricity in the village, plus we'll have roads and even streetlights because you see, we want to be like Europeans and that'll take time and lots of effort, but we'll get there, so anyway, right now I need to smoke this cigarette. Got a light?

4

Mohammed handed all bureaucratic paperwork to his youngest daughter, who spent hours filling out forms for the welfare and health insurance agencies, the bank, and the tax authorities. Although Mohammed had learned the alphabet back in Koranic school and could write his name in Arabic, his signature was a drawing of a tree—an olive tree, he said, the very one (and the only one) that grew in his village. He drew two vertical lines topped with a circle full of crosshatching: an original signature, unlike the traditional X used by his friends.

I can't write, but I like to draw. The children don't know this; they'd make fun of me, so I draw in secret. Don't need school for that. In fact, I have a notebook full of drawings, which I'll leave to my children or, rather, to my grandchildren. I draw trees and houses. That's all. Trees with fruits of every color, big trees, middle-size ones, squat ones, trees thin as sticks, others that are bushy; I draw groves of them and even a forest, and I can walk in the forest, lose my way, stop and sit down with my back against an immense tree trunk, and though I don't know the name of this tree, it offers cool shade to rest in, gives me fresh air, and it does me good, this tree that exists only in the forest I draw, for I know it doesn't exist anywhere else. I draw trees and forests because we don't have any back home, up country where it's all dust and stones, dryness everywhere, and among the large or small stones there are scorpions that sting children while they sleep so that they die asphyxiated, sometimes, when people forget to raise the beds high enough, as with my four-year-old niece who was killed by a scorpion one night: in the morning she was swollen, her eyes shut, she had stopped breathing. If only we'd had water, some small streams, the scorpion wouldn't have stung my little niece.

I draw playgrounds, slides, mazes in an English garden like the one I saw one day on the TV: the whole movie took place among these crisply trimmed rows of trees, where all the grass was as smooth as carpet—I can't remember anymore what the characters said. They wore old-fashioned clothes. It was pretty, orderly, strange. I draw the automobile plant seen from a distance, all splashed with phosphorescent colors, looking like an amusement park with lights that never stop twinkling; I also draw houses with roof terraces free of all satellite dishes and television antennas, terraces draped with rugs and fabrics of shimmering hues. I don't appear to like color, and my children have often reproached me for always wearing gray, but really I adore natural colors, the tints of spring, and I don't need to wear them on my back because they're in my head, where they make music when my mind is tired but they stay inside me, that's why people say I'm sad, but being sad is being frustrated: nothing happens the way I'd hoped, so since I can't do a thing about it, I keep my face closed up tight and watch the world run around as if it were in a frenzy or had some incurable fever, and I've been sad ever since I came to France, a country that has nothing to do with my sorrow but hasn't managed to make me smile, to give me reasons to be happy, that's simply how it is, I can't help it and I'm not the only one—look at the men when they leave the plant, they're all sad, especially ours, the guys from the Maghreb, leaning slightly forward while they walk as if weighed down, although perhaps I'm imagining things and they aren't sad but spending their time having fun, while me, I just can't. So yes, I love colors and I keep that to myself. I can't make my children understand it, but I don't even try, don't feel like talking, explaining myself.

That's why I've never talked much with them. I thought it would be easier for us to talk in France, but even around the dinner table I feel as if they're elsewhere, already gone and merely showing up. Nothing happens. They chat among themselves about their friends, their plans. I don't understand, and a few polite words are all we exchange. But I'm not the only one in this fix. Did my father talk to me? It's true, he didn't say a lot to me, but I knew what had to be done. No need for big speeches. He taught me the fundamentals of our religion: My son, Islam is simple: you alone are responsible for yourself before God, so if you are good you will find goodness in the afterlife, and if you are bad you'll find that instead. There's no mystery: everything depends on how you treat people, especially the weak, the poor, so Islam, that means you pray, you address the Creator and don't do evil around you, don't lie, don't steal, don't betray your wife or your country, don't kill—but do I really need to remind you of this? My mother said nothing, rarely spoke. The day I told her I should get married, she replied, I've thought about that and found you the wife we need. She emphasized the "we." As expected, I married my cousin—a distant cousin—and everything was fine. No trouble, never a harsh word, everything quiet; she has never opposed me, and I have never troubled her. My mother knew what I needed; I'll be eternally grateful to her. Parents should always be trusted, for they know better than their children what's best for them. That's not always true, I know: times change, but I don't. With my children, I couldn't manage it. I don't understand—I'm lost and don't know what to do. I allowed things to happen and said nothing. That wasn't a good solution. Children need to hear their parents, and there I think I made a mess of it. But that's another story, between LaFrance and me.

I never dreamed about LaFrance. True, I heard about people who left to find work in LaFrance, but that's all. When they came back they never talked about LaFrance, just the cold, the difficult language, the people who never smiled at you. They brought back money, though, and things we didn't necessarily need. I remember my uncle who brought home an electric oven and an iron. He'd forgotten that we don't have electricity and use candles and kerosene lamps, and butane gas bottles to run the TV. They used the oven for a pantry. It was so funny! My aunt took precious care of it, wrapped it in an embroidered shawl, and no one else could touch it. The iron was useful for flattening dough to make perfectly thin crêpes. A nephew brought back some underwear, silk bras, but his mother had never worn them and hung them on a nail, saving them for his future fiancée, except that no young woman wanted him because he stuttered, and children made fun of him. When he was angry his stuttering upset him even more, and everyone just laughed louder. He said that in France no one mocked him and the next time he'd go spend his vacation with some peasants in Brittany! He never came back to the village—we lost touch with him.

When I was little my dream was to learn the Koran inside out, to understand it completely, maybe even explain it to others. I recited whole suras yet could not completely grasp their meaning. Nobody in the village could interpret this flood of images. The recitation would excite me so much that I would stutter a little like my cousin, swallowing words so that some vanished down my throat; others left only fragments because they were too long to hold on to. I had other dreams but never dared speak of them. I didn't want to be rich; I just wanted enough money to give presents. Whenever I gazed at the horizon, at that dry mass of red and gray rock, my dreams were too intimidated to show their faces; I feared they might become stuck in that barren landscape, so hard and hopeless. Everything was exaggerated in that place: cold and heat, light and storms, the stars that swarmed in infinite numbers on some nights, and the clouds that blanketed the sky without shedding the tiniest drop of rain. So the dreams stayed sleeping in a cave I never dared to explore. I was scared of what I might find. Dreams, they're like memories: I don't know where they go or where they hide. One of my children once asked me, Where does the light hole up during the day? I thought, That's the sort of question I'd never have asked my father. It was my son who told me the answer: The earth turns, the light stays put, and us, we move with the earth. That was the time when my children asked me questions even if I didn't answer. Now they barely look at me.

Neither Brahim (may God keep his soul in his mercy!) nor Lahcen nor Hamdouch nor Larej nor even Ahmed (who wanted to be called Tony) nor lots of others—none of us asked for citizenship, which we left to the young people, because us, we'll never be one hundred percent Frenchified. Let's be honest, that's not our thing. We're Moroccans, Algerians, Tunisians, Libyans—we're not going to pretend, just to get some documents, and it's not good when guys who can't even speak correctly call themselves French, putting on that TV-announcer accent.

All my children are French, on paper, which at first I had a hard time accepting. I had to sign documents; I hesitated, and we talked about it, my pals and I, but couldn't agree among ourselves. Rabi'i even hit his two daughters with a belt after they filled out the citizenship forms, and they raised a huge stink: the police and press got involved and the girls weren't minors anymore, so poor Rabi'i almost went to prison for assault, but to him their becoming French meant he was publicly admitting that his children didn't belong to him anymore, that LaFrance had taken them under her wing and he had no more say in the matter. All fired up, a reporter stormed the projects with a camera, to hear what he had to say for himself, and ambushed the poor man in a café, where he didn't know *what* to say or how to escape her trap: she bombarded him with questions without giving him time to think, accusing him of every evil plaguing immigrant society, and he was so miserable after this ordeal that he left for Algeria with the youngest of his children, enrolled him in an Algerian high school, and thought, At least they won't get this one.

But things didn't work out the way he'd planned. The kid

ran away, back to Yvelines, where he fell in with a gang of young guys with beards, who were French but wanted to defend the honor of Islam on Christian soil. Even though they knew squat about the Koran, they observed rituals they didn't much understand. The boy was troubled by his predicament: between this band of bearded youths trying to brainwash him and his family with their violent arguments, he no longer knew where he belonged. One day he couldn't take it anymore and shouted, I don't believe in God! The "brothers" started praying to drive Satan away from him, while he just sneered, provoking them with taunts: In the name of your god, they're cutting the throats of little girls in Algeria! Then he bolted and took up with a bunch of petty thieves and drug dealers led by his cousin, known as One Eye. When the cousin died in a car accident, the boy took over for him and grew rich. He kept changing his name and address until he was forced to flee and wound up in Australia, where people say he opened a restaurant called the Couscous King. That's the last we heard of him. His father was so shaken by despair that he stopped speaking and shut himself up in a long silence to wait for his deliverance in death.

5

My children are Mourad, Rachid, Jamila, Othmane, Rekya, and the marvelous Nabile, who is actually the son of my sister, who entrusted him to me in the hope he might get into a school for retarded children. Nabile is my favorite. He was born with a problem, and I believe he has transformed this problem into something wonderful. I'm told he's a "Mongolian," whatever that means, but I know he's an astonishing boy. He throws himself into my arms, hugs me tightly, and says "iluvyoo." My children never tell me that. I don't say it either, actually—that's not the sort of thing the family says at home. Once a secretary at the factory handed me back a form that wasn't properly filled out, so I said, But *he* filled it out; I'm sure he's right. And she said, Who's he? My youngest daughter! The woman was shocked, but how can I explain, that's how it is with us. We don't talk about our daughters or their mother, it's a question

of respect, but the secretary didn't get it. I've never compli-
mented my girls; it isn't done, to say, You are beautiful, my
daughter. No, that we don't do.

My children have Arab features and gestures, but they claim
they are "assimilated," a word I've never understood. One day
Rachid showed me a card and said, With this, I vote. I'm French
and European too. So I said, Hold on: you already waited more
than a year and a half to get your papers; you're not going to start
the same nonsense so you can call yourself European! Don't forget where you come from, where your parents come from; it's
important: wherever you go, always remember that your native
land is written on your face, and it's there whether you like it
or not. Me, I never had any doubt about my country; you kids
today, you don't know what country you're from, and yes, you
say you've been Frenchified, but I think you're the only ones
who believe that—you think the police treat you like a 100 percent Frenchman? True, if you go to court the judge will say
you're French, he has to, but he considers you a foreigner, or else
a bastard. It's as if LaFrance had a bushel of babies with someone from someplace else and then forgot to declare them; what
I mean is *recognize* them. It's very strange, but in any case nothing
is going to be easy for you! When we arrived, there were already
immigrants, from Italy, Spain, Portugal, and they gave us more
or less the fish eye. Actually, they weren't really immigrants like

before, their countries were all going to join Europe and we, we got left at the station, I mean on the sidewalk. It was all right for us to be here, but we had to be discreet, not talk or move around too much. Then one day—I hadn't been here long—the Algerians, who were fighting for their independence, decided to demonstrate in the streets of Paris. I wasn't there, but I know that lots of rooms rented by Algerians were left empty after the demonstration. Their tenants were dead. We whispered about it and were afraid because the police were constantly lurking around the projects.*

Don't ever forget where you come from, my son. Tell me: is it true that you call yourself Richard? Richard Ben Abdallah! It doesn't go together, you've fiddled with the first name, but the family name betrays you: Ben Abdallah, "son of the worshiper of Allah"! That's silly! What did you do? Changed that name too? Ah, I see: you got rid of the servant part and kept just the Ben. Now people might take you for a Jew, that's it, you want to erase your roots and find yourself a spot, a little corner among the French, the Jews preferably, and tell me, is it working? Is it easier for you to find a job? You did that to get into a nightclub? He didn't answer me, ran off. Richard! To think I had a fine sheep slaughtered on the day he was baptized! Rachid is more beautiful than Richard, but what can I do? I'm lucky he didn't erase his father completely like Abdel Malek, our neighbor's son, who left with an American family and sent no news for ten years until the day he turned up back home, calling himself Mike Adley and speaking Berber with a foreign accent. He was ridiculous and didn't even know that his mother was dead. He saw his father, gave him some dollars, and then said good-bye, like some tourist, before vanishing again. Adley! Mike Adley!

What is it they find so attractive in these modern countries? Perhaps it's our way of life that puts them off. They don't like us anymore. We're no longer cool; we're behind the times. They feel ashamed of us. I have never in my life committed an offense, never lied or cheated or stolen. I have always been upright, openhearted, with nothing to hide. I worked so my family would lack nothing, I always gave them presents, vacations, I was an honest father, too honest. My children don't want to be like me. That's the problem. But do I want to be like me?

I locked myself in the bathroom and stared in the mirror for a long while. I saw someone else, old before his time, a face marked by hard work and many years. What have I done with my life? I worked every day, and I slept the rest of the time to recover from work. It's a life the same color as my gray overalls. I never wondered whether my life might have had other colors. When I'm back in Morocco, I don't ask myself all these questions. There I'm in tune with nature even when it's yellow with drought. I'm at home. This feeling has no equal anywhere in the world. How can I put it? It's feeling safe even when storms and lightning threaten, even when there's not enough sugar and water. That's it: here in Yvelines I have never felt at home in our home. It's no one's fault, that's how it is. I'm not accusing LaFrance or Morocco or Jean or Jacques or Marcel or the king or the queen, no: I am not at home where I live. Perhaps my children don't ask themselves that question, so much the better, but that means . . . that I came here so I wouldn't feel at home and they would. But where is it, their home? I've never traveled outside LaFrance; the auto plant committee organizes trips to Italy, Spain, and communist countries, but I've never wanted to leave my children to spend a few days discovering other cities, I've never felt the need. Maybe I should have traveled. I don't know what it's like to be foreign, a tourist in a foreign country; I haven't the time to do things like that.

Fortunately, Nabile is here. Nabile, a gift from God, a light in my life. Like me, he doesn't read well and writes with difficulty, but there's something enchanting about him. He's an angel. When he enters a room, he can spot right away those people who make faces or won't accept his condition. He ignores them. He's incapable of having negative feelings. To me, he has been more than a son: a compass, a guide, sunshine in my gray life, a smile that wipes away a world of woe. I like to go out with him to a restaurant. He loves to dress up and have fun. It's for him that I put on a tie. He insists on that. Without him, I think my life would have been even more difficult and dispiriting. I thank God for sending him to us. When he goes back home to the village, he talks constantly to his parents, telling them about his life with words that no one understands, but he knows that, so he expresses himself with gestures, and then he gets them laughing. He's a clown, a comedian, he's a real actor, by the way, he loves putting on a show, doing magic tricks, acrobatics, and he's so limber and inventive that everyone's astonished. I believe that if he'd stayed in the village he'd be a vegetable today, drooling, with no zest for life. Back home we don't do a thing for such children, just leave them to nature, like animals; no one hurts them, but no one takes care of them, either. In LaFrance he's been to school, played sports, learned music; he's happy.

I'm afraid for him. One day he was the one who said to me: I'm afraid for you. He said it quite clearly. He may be the only one in the family who has understood me. He'd noticed I was glum, pensive, dejected. It brought tears to my eyes. Afraid for me! He's right: sometimes I too am afraid for my health, my mental equilibrium. I may be silent, but I'm thinking, I think all the time, which doesn't show, so my wife, poor woman, doesn't know all this and cannot understand how unhappy I am, but I don't want to upset her. She's a good mother who lives only for her children, as I do, even though I've begun to realize that something is wrong. Then I remember Nabile, and the sun comes out again in my heart. He's the only child in the family who brightens my Sundays.

At a school assembly, his principal once announced that he was on the honor roll. Nabile was pleased, but expectant, and finally asked, So where's the roll? Everyone laughed, and so did he. He'd done it on purpose, to add some fun. At home my youngest daughter has paid the most attention to him. She's deeply fond of this gentle, sensitive boy. Another time he got into a fight during recess because a boy called him a Mongol, and he taught that kid a lesson.

Nabile is athletic, well built, muscular, and good-looking. He doesn't think of himself as handicapped and likes to help people. When he sees someone having trouble walking, he'll take an arm and escort that person across the street. He has hidden gifts. One day we were at Marcel's place. Suddenly we heard somebody playing the piano—and not a beginner, either, just hitting any old keys. It was Nabile, who had quietly sat down at the instrument and begun improvising, to the delight and amazement of us all. He's an independent boy, meticulous, a bit of a perfectionist.

6

I watched the elections, when Le Pen sprang his big surprise on Chirac, and I had a good laugh, but my wife was afraid and wondered if we should start packing.* No, I said, don't worry, Le Pen needs us, oh yes. Imagine this country emptied of its immigrants, when he could no longer blame all evil and uncertainty on us, claiming that we're taking advantage of social security and child benefits! He'd be in a fix without Arabs to pick on. No, he's putting on his usual act. He'll never get any real power, but who knows, politics—sometimes I watch it on TV, and when they talk about us it's a bad sign. No one says anything nice about our work. That's how it's always been; I'm used to it.

And you know how I hate suitcases and those huge plastic bags in garish colors from discount stores, "migrant bags" they're called, and I hate packing cases crammed with useless stuff we have to lug along to the village to hand out to the stay-at-homes. I hate luggage, obligatory gifts, junk that piles up in the cellar. I hate things that glitter and aren't worth spit—but you, you're always afraid of running out of something, you carry so much with you that even I begin to wonder if maybe war might break out, if we'd better stock up, so I don't object, I keep quiet, let you do what you want.

Well, anyway, I watched Le Pen: he's scary, he has fat hands, and slaps from those hands must make a guy see stars, fake stars, but I can't take him seriously, I don't know why; he makes me laugh, and I always imagine him in rather unflattering positions, the nasty kind, yet I know there are other Le Pens in this country who may not talk the way he does but they don't like us just the same, and how come? *How come no one likes us?* What terrible thing did we do to be objects of suspicion and even abuse in the street? Our reputation isn't exactly spotless, which must come from way back, maybe the Algerian war or even longer ago, and obviously there's the rotten-apple-spoiling-the-whole-barrel business, so what can we do? Keep a low profile? We are low-profile experts, my companions and I—we hunker down, don't raise our voices even when we've been the victims of some injustice or everyday racism because we don't want any trouble. What can we do? *Disappear!* Cease to exist, become transparent while still slaving away—in fact, that would be ideal: to be here, being useful, efficient, but invisible, without having children or cooking with our smelly spices, and I've often thought about that, how to be as low-key as possible and work as if we didn't exist. Before, or at least when I came to LaFrance, no one mentioned us; we started off in projects housing immigrant workers, then later hardly ever ventured into town, but when our children came along the noise level rose, and quite a bit, so why attract even more attention by asking for citizenship? I'm fine with my green passport, my ten-year residence permit. I don't need a different color passport.

Seems the people of LaFrance prefer us Moroccans; the poor Algerians, they're out of luck: their country's been occupied for so long, and nowadays Algeria is rich, I saw that on TV. They've got oil and gas, underground treasures that will feed them for centuries, yet they're emigrating—more and more are coming here. It's awful, such a rich country with such poor people! (It's not me saying that but a human rights activist in Algeria.) It's different in Morocco. We're poor and always have been. City people live better than country folk. But us, we have the Makhzen: the *caïd*, the pasha, the governor—representatives of the central power that governs us. We don't know how it works, but the police and the army do whatever the Makhzen wants. The poor person has no rights, submits, and keeps quiet. Whoever hollers gets "disappeared." That's the Morocco I left in 1960, to take the train then the boat then the train to Lalla França. I never talked politics. I know, however, that both sons of the butcher in Imintanout went missing. A couple of plainclothesmen who said they were from the Darkoum Real Estate Agency asked the two young men to show them some land their father had for sale, and the car they drove off in had a temporary license plate even though it was basically a jalopy. The youths never returned. The father went to Marrakech to find the agency, which had never existed. The mother went mad, and the father shut up shop. That was in the summer of 1966. They were high school kids in Marrakech. Whenever I visited in the summer, people would tell me about all the youngsters in prison, almost whispering even though there was no one near us.

Fear, yes, I have known fear. Fear that they would take away my precious passport, fear that I would be arrested for no reason. That happened to Lahcen, who was held in the police station at the airport for more than two days; they had forgotten him. When they gave him back his passport, the officer said, Since you're lucky to live over there, think of your brother, empty your pockets—we have to help one another, it's only natural, because some have everything and others almost nothing but suffering, and you won't let your brother suffer, so take a hint, my friend! Lahcen gave him whatever money he had and left the police station suffering from a wicked migraine.

Fortunately, that Morocco no longer exists. It's over, the time of fear, when the Makhzen acted without respect for the law and what's right. I discovered this going through customs in Tangier. Overnight the customs agents had become polite, no longer suspecting us of smuggling drugs or weapons. It seems the new king ordered them to stop harassing us. He's a good fellow, this young king, not at all like his father.* At the time, some of our immigrants worked for the consulate or the police in Rabat, and we could identify them because they would loudly criticize the king and the government. Me, I always said Long live the king, long live Morocco! Then they had nothing to report to their bosses. It was Marcel, the union rep, who warned me: You know, watch out. That Sallam, the guy who just arrived from Roubaix, well, he never worked there; he came directly from Rabat and funnels information about the Moroccan immigrant community to the police. There's him and the other one, the really skinny guy who calls himself FelFla, "Pepper."

The CGT, the labor union federation, has always helped us. They're the ones who organized literacy classes on Saturdays and Sundays at the Labor Exchange, run by young students from Paris and French-speaking guys from our cities—Fez, Marrakech, Casablanca—who would take turns coming to teach us. We enjoyed those afternoons, found them relaxing—we'd talk about home; our teachers explained things; sometimes the French students would help us write letters to our families and, most importantly, fill out official forms for our retirement, bank accounts, and so on. Even if I did have trouble learning the language, I preferred being there to spending the day in a café, watching people come and go. At my age, learning to read is no joke. I did pick up driving pretty easily, though. I'd stare at the signs and imprint them in my head. I've always been a prudent man. I know the highway code by heart. Where I run into trouble, it's with detours: there I screw up and choose some road that takes me back to where I came from. Roadwork and those detours, they terrify me. I know the France–Morocco trip by heart. I never speed. I stop now and then for rest breaks. I get backaches, so I do exercises. Often it's having to pee that makes me pull over. That's how we found out I've got the sugar—a young Moroccan doctor explained to me about diabetes. Now I'm careful, although back home I do let myself go, I admit. That's what it's for: letting go, not worrying, forgetting about rules. It's hard to say no to a glass of our sweetened mint tea; that hurts people's feelings, so I drink the tea and ask God to help me deal with all that extra sugar in my blood.

Brahim wouldn't learn to read or write. He liked to drink beer and frequented Khadija, the whore who dyed her hair blond and called herself Katy. She wasn't a bad woman, but she'd lost all her teeth, poor thing, in a fight with her pimp, and she worked as the cleaning lady in the bar where Brahim hung out. She was pitiful. Men didn't want her anymore, so she drank to console herself, and on Saturdays she'd set herself up on the sidewalk at the Saint-Ouen flea market and use henna to "tattoo" girls' arms and hands. She had a gift for delicately tracing arabesques on their skin.

Mohammed knew Khadija's story but kept his distance, more from timidity than from any moral or religious disapproval. One day she came over to him as if she were drowning and desperate for help. He didn't know what to do, especially when she kissed his hand. Seeing the anguish in her face, he slipped her some money, because he considered her an unlucky casualty of immigration. Then he thought about it and decided that her lot was her fate, that she would have gone bad even if she'd never left home. Everything is written. Nothing happens by chance—yet he also knew that people are responsible for their actions. He stopped and thought: If I go into this bar, get staggering drunk, and lose my human dignity, I am the guilty one, not God. If I do something stupid and make a ton of foolish mistakes, it's my fault and mine alone; let's leave God out of it. So if I keep walking along, if I slip on a banana peel and break my back, is it God who wanted me to crack in two? Or is the guilty guy the bastard who threw away the banana peel without a thought for passersby who might snap their spines? No: one must simply be careful and watch one's step. But after our 'tirement, aren't we left in a bad way, in an unhealthy and woeful state? I mean, my muscles ache even though I don't work anymore, my joints hurt, and my body feels battered by a strange fatigue, a tiredness I've never felt before, and it's weird, because it comes from nothing: the nothingness that has taken over my life is beginning to eat away at my body. Life is hollowing me out. I'm in pain. I don't complain, that's not my style, but ever since I caught 'tirement, nothing goes right. I used to like my tiredness at day's end when I came home. While I washed up, my wife would fix me a light supper; I'd see the children, and during the TV news programs drowsiness would steal over me. I'd fall into bed and a deep sleep. Now I miss that beautiful exhaustion. In its place is a more insidious, disturbing fatigue. I must be ill. One day the doctor at work told us, Listen carefully: if you wake up tired in the morning, that's because something is wrong, it's the sign of a hidden illness that doesn't dare show itself. Maybe that's it. But I don't feel like consulting a doctor.

I'm a little ashamed when I think that I still rose at dawn when my 'tirement began, put on my work overalls, took my lunch box, and went off to the factory. It was automatic—I couldn't break free of those actions I'd made part of my life, my body, my soul. (May God forgive me; I shouldn't bring my soul into all this.) I'd get to the factory gate, stop short, and watch my comrades go in: happy, joking around, ready for a long and good day's work. I felt mortified. They didn't understand why I kept coming back, and I didn't feel like talking to them, explaining or justifying myself to anyone. Then there's my wife. She didn't say anything but gave me peculiar looks. What was I going to do now with my gray overalls, my lunch box, my protective goggles, my papers, my endless days off, all this time crashing down on me like a pile of rubble? I can't even bequeath it all to one of my children—not that they've noticed that I've fallen into 'tirement. They ask me no questions, drop by briefly and head out again without paying any attention to how I feel. Watching them, I can't manage to see their own children treating them the same way. Everything changes. It's hard to accept that we can find ourselves so quickly in a different world. Our forefathers didn't prepare us, told us nothing. They'd never have imagined that men would leave their land to go abroad.

When Mohammed thought about it, he became convinced that 'tirement had killed Brahim. He'd seen him wandering the streets, drinking at Katy's place, stumbling and weaving whenever he decided to go home. His wife had gone back to Morocco, influenced by that same Allam who'd had a hold on Mohammed's wife and eldest daughter; the man was a marriage counselor as well as a sorcerer, and he'd encouraged Brahim's wife to go home to her village to protect herself against that man-eating witch Khadija: You see, she's a wreck, poor thing, so you'd best avoid her, take your husband and go back home where at least there's no bar, no alcohol, no Katy. Your husband is bored, and now that he no longer works he's always shacked up with that pitiful woman, but you, if you want to get your man back, you must take things boldly in hand. Here is a talisman to put in your purse and here's another to sew into the inside pocket of Brahim's jacket: these should help the both of you. But as you know, everything is in the hands of Almighty God!

Brahim refused to follow his wife. He found, tore up, and stamped on the bit of cloth sewn into his jacket. You tried to cast a spell on me? Well, I piss on it, your spell! Go, get out! Go back home to your parents, leave me alone. I'm tired.

Brahim found himself all alone in their half-empty apartment. Dirty laundry piled up in a corner of the living room. His wife had taken the family photos, but one picture remained, hanging on a wall, a photograph of a snowy landscape, perhaps some Swiss or Canadian mountains, and it was nice to look at in that apartment stripped of every reminder of his native land. Both his children lived and worked abroad and used to call now and then, until the phone was cut off. Unpaid bills, unopened letters. Brahim was letting himself fall apart. When he had a liver attack and screamed in pain, neighbors called a doctor, who sent him to the hospital. There he called for his children, whose phone numbers were in a notebook, but he had no idea where it was. The pain was so awful he couldn't remember things from moment to moment. When Mohammed came to visit, he found him frighteningly pale, thin, with jaundiced eyes and dry lips. Brahim had lost the will to live. Mohammed told him their religion forbade that and recited a few verses from the Koran that he knew by heart. Gripping the patient's arm, he bent to kiss him on the forehead, and when he straightened up, tears coursed down his cheeks. After staying a moment longer, Mohammed went on his way, thinking about his own death. So much loneliness, ingratitude, and silence left him speechless. Where had the man's brothers gone, his friends, his companions in misfortune? Was that how immigrants took leave of this world? That solitude stank like a mixture of medicine and whatever was stalking them, these poor souls whom no one had warned about the way they would end their lives.

7

Mohammed was thinking about his retirement again and feeling sick. When his saliva dried up, he would drink a few glasses of water. It wasn't diabetes that was attacking his body but his recent retirement, the idea of retirement, which obsessed him, bringing him dark visions. The Chaabi bank, on the avenue de Clichy, had just sent him the annual form to renew his insurance for "repatriation of the body," and Mohammed took it as a sign, a bad coincidence. Haunted by his fear of dying far from his native land, he saw himself draped in a white sheet at the morgue, his body lying there for several days due to administrative problems, and then he saw himself in a coffin, sent to Morocco with other merchandise, and his friends collecting money for the family—he saw all this in such detail that his skin crawled.

No, me, I'm not going home in a box, not like Brahim, no,

I'll get the jump on death and wait for it calmly in my village, I'm not afraid of it, I'm a believer, and whatever happens is always God's will: God alone decides the hour of death, I'm sure of that, it's written, and I even think it's all settled for us on the twenty-seventh night of Ramadan, a sacred night, worth more than a thousand months, so for death, I'll arrange to escape the box, because even if I'm dying I'll take the plane—and I hate planes—to die at home, not with strangers, foreigners who know nothing of my religion, my traditions.

Aha! you'll tell me. And your children? Well, that's a sore point, very sore. No, my children will be saddened, but would they escort me back home? Would they wash my body in the Muslim way? If I'm buried in the village, will they come pay their respects at my tomb? Perhaps at first, but later they won't bother to come all that way to visit a grave overgrown with weeds, strewn with plastic bags, empty bottles, old newspapers thrown there by visitors without any sense of propriety. Lots of Moroccans leave their litter in cemeteries as if the dead had no right to clean graves. I can't see my children gathering to remember their father on some Friday just before the noonday prayer, raising their hands, palms pressed together, and reciting a few verses from the sura "Al-Baqara" to ask God to have mercy on my soul.* I don't see them spending any vacation time to perform such seemingly useless actions. That doesn't mean they wouldn't ever think of me; they'll remember me in their own way, any way they like, but they'll remember me. When I visit my parents' graves, I get the shivers; I sit on a large stone and talk to them the way I used to, telling them about my life and the people they loved, going into detail, especially for my mother, who was always eager for news—I can still hear her demanding to know the name of the grocer's fiancée and how many children he had with his first wife, and asking if my aunt is still so stingy and bad tempered and her children still dirty and greedy. I imagine all that and I smile. I love that ritual. Then I go pray at the little mosque and give alms.

Oh, enough of these black ideas—my children will never leave me! I'd rather not think that they might ever forget me. Last year a poor Algerian fellow was buried in Bobigny, where they had a hard time finding him a tiny spot in the Muslim cemetery. His children didn't want to send his body back to his village: they said that Algeria wasn't their country anymore and France wasn't either, so what did it matter in which hole they buried the body? What counts is the soul, in any case, and once it leaves the body it goes off to God. But I wouldn't like to leave my body in a French hole. It's foolish, what I'm saying, but if I could be certain that my children would often visit my grave if I were buried in France, no problem, I'd give my body to Lalla LaFrance; I'd make things simpler for them.

I'll be frank: black or gray thoughts aside, deep down I'd

like my kids to come back home to gather a few Koranic readers at my tomb in my village, on a Friday, preferably, and they
should give a little money to the many beggars. For some time
now, it's been Africans who beg around cemeteries. Poor
things, they left their homelands to come work in Europe.
They walked day and night, and then were abandoned. They
beg to survive. They aren't pushy; some of them are embar-
rassed to have sunk to this. Ever since I stopped working I've
been obsessed by such ideas. Death, Hallab told me—he's the
one who claims to be an imam—death is nothing, you don't
feel anything anymore, and it's as if you were sound asleep. If
it's nothing, I asked him, how come everyone is so afraid?
If you're at peace with yourself, he replied, and have nothing
to reproach yourself for, you will be happy to go to God, whose
infinite heavens are full of goodness and mercy. Hallab's a fine
fellow, but what does he know? He repeats what's in the Koran.
I will never contradict the Koran, but I confess that sometimes, at night, I sit up with a start, drenched in sweat, and I
see death. It isn't a skeleton with a scythe, or an old lady all in
black, either: no, death is an odor, a strong, asphyxiating odor
announced by an icy draft that lifts the sheets to flow over the
body trembling with cold, while the feet, growing numb with
pins and needles, become rigid. I've imagined death so much
that it can't play any tricks on me. I know death; I saw it in
Brahim's face, I know what it looks like and how it operates.

On that score, I feel calm. I know it's still a ways off from my bedroom, far away from my life.

Hallab had found the solution: to pass himself off as a religious expert. So then religion helps us to leave this world behind? Of course: man is weak, he is nothing compared to the immensity of divine grandeur.

Hallab would talk and talk to me, quoting verses of Islamic poetry, but I could never manage to tear my thoughts and eyes away from that cheap wooden box I'd wind up in if I died abroad. Ever since I can remember, I've heard that we belong to Allah and to him we will return. That's what we say over the body whenever we bury a Muslim. I belong to God, I am his property, and he takes it back when he pleases. There is no reason to be afraid or feel humiliated, no: death is not a humiliation even if it makes us angry, for we must understand that our anger is like a wisp of smoke, a bit of mist wafting up into the sky.

Personally, sickness is what frightens me. Suffering before going—that would be unbearable. Plus we say that the true believer, the man faithful to God, is often exposed to affliction and even injustice: *al mouminou moussab*. I don't understand why good Muslims, righteous, honest, never straying from God's path, would endure a harsher fate than crooks. And God knows *they're* all over the place. They do well, make money without working, fill their bellies with other people's goods, enjoy wonderful health, eat more than everyone else, say, *Al hamdou lillah! A chokro lillah!* [Blessings and thanks be to Allah!], then belch with self-satisfaction. I see them everywhere, those thieves disguised as men of good family; they are legion, and nothing ever happens to them, not even a tiny migraine or the slightest indisposition; they sleep well, do sports, and give the *zakat*, the 10 percent Islam assigns to charity.

I'll never forget the guy from Marrakech, sent, he claimed, by the Ministry of Water and Electricity to collect a tax to fund the installation of meters, thanks to which our women and children would finally get to wash in running water. He amassed a goodly sum, gave us receipts, lots of forms with the official heading, and that was the last we saw of him. A stocky man with malice in his eyes, smiling and laughing like a hyena, who spoke with the Marrakech accent. He had some sample meters in his van, and we all fell into his trap. He pulled the same scam in the neighboring village. Never got arrested. Even better: I think I saw him on a Moroccan TV news program in the entourage of a minister of public works. It had to be him: that laugh, his squashed face, the little chin tuft—that was his trademark. The sign of Satan's spawn.

I am not a wicked man, but I'm a devotee of justice, cannot bear to see it perverted, and I do sometimes dream of vengeance. I would love to see that toadlike thief in the hands of the law, then released in our village where everyone would be waiting to demand their money back. I'd enjoy seeing him stripped of everything and imprisoned for life. Personally, I would have set him out in the sun in a cage with no food or water, long enough for him to learn what a daily ordeal it is to thirst for water and go without. But God will punish him! At least I hope so. Ah, divine retribution! Sometimes it's magnificent, arriving in time to show that anyone who despoils the poor of what little they have will taste God's wrath, watched by the victims. Doesn't happen often, though; seems we have to be patient, learn how to wait while God tests us, and not render evil for evil but believe in his justice, for he avenges the robbed and betrayed orphan, and all who are wronged. If I were to meet that jolly Marrakechi dwarf and have the chance to run him over with my jalopy, would I? The thought of seeing him in agony is tempting, I admit, but I'm losing my mind: bastards are better left in the hands of God.

At the auto plant, the French and Portuguese workers welcomed the day when they could finally enjoy their leisure time, take trips, putter around the house and garden, read, even work on their own projects. They made plans, organized their lives as "young retirees." As Marcel said: At sixty years we're barely two-thirds of the way through our lives, so why bury ourselves? Life is for living!

Marcel had arrived in France right after the war; he must have been all of ten years old. A bon vivant, a champion drinker and talker, he was the scourge of the shop foremen. Of Polish birth, a Jew and an atheist, he sympathized with the Palestinian cause and didn't understand why the Arab states were doing nothing for their brothers in the occupied territories. When Mohammed, who grieved over the Palestinians' fate, said he couldn't figure out politics at all, Marcel offered to teach him, but Mohammed wouldn't budge; even thousands of miles from his village, he still feared the Makhzen. It was in France that he heard about human rights for the first time and learned as well that in his own country men died under torture or rotted in prison without benefit of trial. Marcel kept him up-to-date, telling him, Your country is marvelous, but it's in the hands of some unsavory characters: the Moroccan police were trained by the French, who taught them how to torture, but the Moroccan system is based on fear, and even you are afraid. I understand you: you're scared of being arrested when you go back home. It's the same thing in Algeria, Tunisia—as soon as you protest against the politics of repression you're done for and they pick you up at the border; that's why immigrants don't move around much. You, you keep quiet, and I know that what goes on in your country pains you.

Mohammed remembered the Koranic school and drifted off in distant memories of days when everything was simple, when he didn't even know there were roads, tall buildings, lampposts illuminating streets where no one lived. The world was as big as his village. He had trouble imagining anywhere else. One's native land always leaves a bitter aftertaste. Mohammed's country was dry, bare; it had nothing, and this nothing had followed him even to France. This nothing was important. He had no choice: he couldn't exchange it for another nothing that was perhaps a little more colorful, better equipped. He made do, with patience and resignation. In the end he'd stopped wondering about all that. What the police got up to in their far-off stations, well, he couldn't imagine, and his village was light-years away from the city.

Did he want to live like the French? He considered his fellow workers at the plant and didn't envy their lot. Each to his own life and way of life. He didn't criticize them but was puzzled by how they treated their parents and children. The spirit of family, as he saw it, was no longer honored in France. This slippage shocked him. He just couldn't understand why girls smoked and drank in front of their parents and went out at night with boys. And why did huge billboards display half-naked women to sell perfumes or cars? Most of all, he was afraid for his own family and talked this over with his pals. They sighed, raising their arms to heaven in resignation. What could you do?

One Sunday he invited Marcel home to dinner. It was a holiday, and Mohammed told him, Bring your wife but no wine! Marcel agreed to skip his wine and merrily stuffed himself with the good things fixed by Mohammed's wife. Marcel liked to tell his friend, Time, it's us. It isn't the watch face, no. It's you who make time: when you close your eyes you're in the past; when you close them again you project yourself into the future; when you decide to open them it's no mystery that you're in the present, the one that's as thin as cigarette paper. You follow me?

Before going home to their families after their weekend French lessons, some of the plant workers went to see women in trailers and waited their turn shamefacedly. Mohammed had always refused this kind of distraction. He was afraid of diseases and of what his friends and neighbors might say. Something like a curtain of fog half veiled one late-afternoon memory, on a Sunday when boredom had played out in what Mohammed considered a bestial instinct. He'd been dragged along by an acquaintance whose name he had forgotten and who told him, Listen, if you don't empty your balls now and then, it goes up to your brain and you go blind. Another time he said, Even our religion allows us to empty our balls: you simply write out a document and tear it up afterward. You know, the marriage for pleasure. You get married long enough to fornicate, then you divorce, and you're all square with God and morality.* Mohammed had chuckled to himself and gone off with his chatty companion.

That Sunday there was hardly any line in front of Suzy's small apartment. A bit fat, as vulgar as they come, Suzy seemed to have made an effort to exaggerate her appearance, as if that were part of whoring, but she was so nice, so human, that everyone overlooked her heavily rouged cheeks, her nauseating perfume, and the alcohol. Her eyes were never still but always vacant; she was there and elsewhere. She knew her work was unusual, and she too was looking forward to retirement because she'd had it with spreading her legs and squeezing immigrant balls. But she liked the men, even found their shyness and awkwardness touching, she said.

Mohammed's guide explained the deal precisely. You go in, you smile at her (she likes men who smile), and you put your hundred francs in a bowl on the night table. There are licorice and mint candies in the bowl—the mint's my favorite—to make your breath sweet, so you take one, and you also take a very thin sheath called a rubber that protects you from diseases and other complications; then you lie down on the bed and let her get to work: she's quick, expert, efficient, and she has a fantastic technique to clean out your balls in a few minutes. You'll see—you'll feel a lot better. If you don't know how to put on the rubber, she'll take care of it, don't worry, and when it's over, hey, you'll thank your pal!

The fog thickened; Mohammed hung his head, trying to chase away those images from so long ago. Still, he did remember that Suzy had been very kind to him. He'd never gone back, though.

He associated this memory with a more unpleasant one, a humiliating experience. The medical officer at the factory,

Dr. Garcia, had been blunt with him when he'd reached fifty: Mohammed, you get up often at night to take a leak? Then you must have prostate problems. We'll have to have a look at that.

At the appointment, the doctor told him to remove his trousers and underpants and to bend over as if he were praying. Mohammed just stood there, shaking his head. Growing impatient, the doctor pretended to suddenly understand, then said, I know, it isn't easy, embarrassment and shame, *hchouma*. I know all about it. But I must examine you, and I can't do it long-distance. Just trust me: it takes thirty seconds, then it's over, doesn't even hurt. Mohammed would have liked to tell him that it wasn't a question of physical pain, no, but that he'd never shown his rear end to anyone. After a moment, Mohammed closed his eyes, quickly pulled down his trousers and underpants, and bent over. The doctor asked him to bend a little more. Raging inside, Mohammed did so. The doctor performed a rectal exam. Fine, your prostate's a normal size for your age, but we'll have to keep an eye on it, right, Mohammed? Let's have you back here in one year.

When he left, Mohammed walked along staring at the ground. He was angry at himself and sorry he hadn't asked Dr. Garcia to anesthetize him for the exam. And he didn't like the doctor telling him to bend over as if he were praying. He couldn't bear it that a finger had probed his anus. He never mentioned the visit to anyone and from then on ignored his prostate completely.

8

Time. He couldn't have cared less about time. It was an enemy, the one that would be the first to strip him naked before himself and his family. He compared it to a long rope that doesn't always hold. A rope that frays, slips its knots, dangling at the end of a pole. A shroud, but its whiteness is mere illusion. Time could only be too long, painful, without light, without joy, a line that rises only to fall, air full of dust. Time had several faces; it was a traitor that would break him gently, then finish him off the way it had his pal Brahim.

Mohammed didn't know how to garden or to tackle projects around the house, and as for traveling, the only trips he'd ever taken, besides the pilgrimage to Mecca, were the ones home from France to his village in southern Morocco. As he liked to say, he drove on and on, covering the 2,882 kilometers within forty-eight hours. He ate up time without speeding. He wanted to be faster and stronger than his opponent. It was a performance, a challenge: he'd get the idea into his head that he was going to beat time, poke holes in it, look it in the face and have a good laugh—and he was a man who never laughed anymore. He liked the fatigue after the drive, a deep, lovely fatigue after a job well done, because once back home, after triumphing over time, he paid no more attention to it. He felt safe, completely safe. Nothing disturbed him, no one bothered him.

He'd sleep through the next day and night. His little prostate problem would interrupt his rest two or three times and, rising to pee, he'd remember Dr. Garcia and that humiliating examination. Mohammed couldn't understand why the doctor had inserted a finger into his anus to check his prostate. Why doesn't he take an X-ray? With that, you see everything. That Garcia must be a pervert. The shame! He should just forget the whole thing. Mohammed thought of Khalid, his cousin's son, who left one day with a Canadian tourist. Rumor had it that he was practically a girl and hid from people because they saw him as abnormal. Boys used to taunt him; some had supposedly even abused him behind the little mountain. Poor Khalid disappeared and hadn't been heard from since. Living with a man, people said. Absolute disgrace! His parents preferred to claim that he was ill and receiving treatment in America. The fact that he sent them money orders put them on the spot. One day his father had yelled, I haven't any son!

Khalid is not my son! He's a bastard I tried to adopt, but Islam is right—adoption is forbidden, and I've been punished!

Each voyage home was an event in the village. Once there, Mohammed always forgot how he hated cumbersome luggage. He loved that atmosphere, that joy in the faces of children eager for presents; he loved those reunions with the old folks, with the members of a huge family who gazed at him, their eyes brimming with envy. The family was the tribe. From the outside, it seemed like an invading, clinging horde. The doors of the houses didn't close, and even if they'd been bolted shut, the tribe would have come in through the windows or down from the roof terrace, respecting no limits, for the tribe was at home anywhere in the village. Not only did everyone know everyone else, but they meddled in one another's affairs. It was a big family organized in an archaic manner, governed by traditions and superstitions. There was nothing Mohammed could do about that; it was in their blood: you can't escape your roots. He wasn't even bothered when certain members of the tribe "misbehaved." His nephew had built a house on some of Mohammed's land, but he didn't reclaim it; that's what family was. When his eldest son, Mourad, protested, Mohammed ended the matter by reminding him that family is sacred and one doesn't quarrel over a scrap of land. You have to fight back when someone takes your property, Mourad had insisted. Nephew, cousin, brother—

if you steal my land, I'll do anything to get it back. I don't understand this kind of one-way solidarity! You think he'd have let you grab some of *his* property? I doubt it!

Confronting the tribe, Mohammed was weak; he knew his complaints would go nowhere. No point in fighting the customs of centuries. His children had almost no connection with all that. And anyway, no one in the village would understand why Mohammed was displeased. The tribe is the tribe. No arguments. No criticism. We're not Europeans here. The family is sacred! That's how it is, and that's that.

Mohammed began to think out loud: But Europeans love their families—they celebrate at Christmas, get together, chat, sing. I spent one Christmas Eve with Marcel's family. They drink too much, though, and I don't like that; everybody drinks: the children drink and get drunk with their parents. I didn't say anything, but I was afraid my kids might one day turn out like Marcel's. They have their customs, we have ours; we're not all obliged to do the same thing. LaFrance is my workplace: the plant, the fumes of plastic, oil, and the paint I used on the endless assembly line. My father smelled of sweat and plowed earth. I smelled of chemicals, an acrid metallic odor I grew used to. But my children didn't come hug me close for fear of a whiff of it—they pecked me on the cheek and said, Hi, Pa!

Aïe! Hi, Pa! Me, I kissed my parents' hands and begged them to bless and forgive me in case I might have done something wrong. Hi, Pa! Sure, hi yourself, sonny!

———————

When his children were still young, they'd gone back to the village with him. They'd amused themselves, played with the animals, tossed rotting chicken guts at the cats to lure them within capturing range, and made toys out of any old thing. They had diabolical imaginations and were quite boisterous, annoying, spoiled, without any self-control. The neighbors said they hadn't been brought up properly, didn't respect anyone or anything! LaFrance was responsible—unless it was the parents' fault, for letting the kids walk all over them. The parents couldn't bear to hear their offspring criticized, however, and blamed that hyperactivity on the vacation itself. As for the children, it never even crossed their minds that they truly belonged to this sprawling clan. They looked after themselves as best they could, ate here or there: every house in the village was open to them. No one thought twice about it. The kids loved the old uncle who claimed to have lived to a hundred thanks to pure honey; they believed him and made themselves honey sandwiches all day long. One even told Mohammed it was almost as good as Nutella!

But after a week or so, they'd grow bored, become aggressive, clamor to go to the beautiful beaches at Agadir. Mohammed would take them there and keep an eye on them from a nearby café. After bringing them back to the village in the evening, he'd feel exhausted but could refuse them nothing. One day his elder sister, Fattouma, asked him, Why don't you slap them? They've got bad manners, those kids, and when they come here they upset our children, teach them things I can't believe—my God, that's it: they're little Frenchies! My baby brother has brought us some little Christians, foreigners.

And then there was young Nabile, who ran everywhere, fell often, hurt himself, but didn't cry. His mother, Fattouma, sometimes called him Malak, "Angel," or Baraka, "God's Gift." This child is different, she'd tell people.

God has sent him to us, a sign of deliverance and future prosperity. We have to let him do as he pleases. He doesn't know what evil is. To him, everyone is good. He walked at two years, talked at three; we couldn't tell what he was saying but could guess what he meant. He made signs, precise gestures to express himself. The midwife told me that I'd eaten too much garlic and that's why Nabile was born special. A young doctor in the hospital in Marrakech tried to explain to me once, telling me things I didn't understand: You're too old to have children, you shouldn't have made this boy, but now you have to live with his slowness. He isn't bad, he'll even be quite affectionate, but it will be tiring. The doctor drew a picture to show me, a kind of branch with twenty-three rows of leaves, right and left, then underlined the twenty-first branch and said: You see, there, three leaves—that's one leaf too many. It's that tiny "too much" that causes the problem. I kept the drawing; I'm waiting for my son who's at university to come home and explain it to me. Nabile is unique. After Koranic school (where he didn't learn a thing), I agreed to give him to my brother Mohammed, who registered him with the state as if he'd been his own son. After everything had been arranged, Mohammed took Nabile off to France, where he goes to a school that has a class just for children like him. He likes school. He learns music, does theater, and plays several sports. If I'd kept him with me, he'd have grown sicker and sicker, and I'd have gone crazy. Fortunately, Mohammed took charge of him. Today he's a tall young man, elegant, funny, intelligent. When he comes back on vacation, he brings me presents and helps me with the housework. He's healthy and especially loving, an angel, a *baraka*. The last time, he insisted I come back with him to France. I told him: I have no passport, no visa, no money! He didn't understand. He grabbed a notebook, scribbled something, and handed it to me, saying, Here, bassbor, isa, and me with you. He made me cry. I hugged him tight and felt his tears trickling down my neck.

Time. When very young, Mohammed had had problems with time. He didn't know what it stood for, and he anchored it on important events during the year, but living to the rhythm of a wristwatch proved difficult because he didn't have one. The day was divided up by the five prescribed prayers. His wristwatch was the sun and its shadow. Mohammed was sometimes able, however, to feel the real weight of time, to imagine it as a load on the back of a hobbling old man. To kill time, Mohammed would take that imaginary burden and kick it around. He'd till the soil especially slowly, and when he went to the mosque, he'd repeat the same prayer a few times. Animals had a better relationship with time, or at least with the rising and setting of the sun. Using the five daily prayers as reference points, Mohammed tried to fill the emptiness around them. Like everyone else in his village, he saw time as little more than something thought up by people in a hurry. He couldn't figure out why they said, Time is money. On that score, he counted himself rich!

One day his cousin, the one who limped because of a work accident in Belgium, suggested they open a shop on the road to Marrakech and sell time. How're you going to do that? asked Mohammed. Simple: I sell tourists *all the time we've got too much of* around here! I know them—I've been around them in Europe. I'll tell them, Come to our country; you'll find lots of time available. There's nothing to do: you'll rest, you won't check your watches anymore, and at day's end you'll wonder where the time went. Clever, no? And he told Mohammed, If you help me, we'll make a fortune! Mohammed replied, Time is wind, the dust in the air, the sun, the moon, the stars, and Joha. You remember Joha—the guy who pretended to be an idiot when we were kids, to make us laugh?

Another time the cousin proposed they sell ready-made memories to tourists. When Mohammed asked him what he meant, the cousin replied, It's simple. (Everything's always simple with him.)

We bring the tourists to the village, invite them to tea, pass a bit of time with them, bring in our centenarian, old Hajji, who'll read their palms while I translate, and then they'll give us a little money for a small piece of sheepskin that will remind them of their visit. That's the memory, the souvenir. The bigger the sheepskin, the more important the memory, hey? . . . You know, Mohammed, you're a real wet blanket; you never believe in anything! It's just impossible to get a business deal going with you. Hey, I've got another idea. You can't disagree with this one, listen: I saw some rich people on the TV, Frenchies or Spanioolies who come to live with poor peasants. It gives them a change from their big buildings, cars, everything we haven't got, so we're going to sell the countryside. It'll be a vacation village for rich people tired of being rich: they'll come to us for the experience of nothing. Us, we've got nothing, no water, no electricity, big nothing, so they'll come to live the way their really ancient ancestors did, going to the well, using candles; they'll eat whatever there is without being allowed to complain, and they'll pay us for it! More and more retirees are settling in Morocco, so a married couple . . . that means two retirees, two monthly checks, enough to live like a government minister—

no, better . . . so we'll go looking for clients among these carefree retirees. Isn't that a great plan? We'll have to go to Marrakech or Agadir to put the ad in their papers.

When I was in the city of Mons, I knew some Belgians who retired and went off to India to be with a flimflam guru— you know, the real skinny kind of guy with a long beard, who sits cross-legged on a seriously uncomfortable mat, gazing into the distance while the Europeans at his feet soak up his silence as if it were a prophet's blessing. Can you imagine, they're ready to swallow just about anything, so I'll take hundred-year-old Hajji, dress him up in a lovely white silk robe, dye his long beard with henna, hand him some prayer beads, and introduce him as the master of patience and silence, and it'll work: they'll come by the hundreds just to smell his perfume and venerate his serenity, plus we'll tell them that Hajji is in communication with what awaits us on the other side, but he also knows how to prepare us to enter that other world, and then you toss in a few verses of the Koran, you burn the herbal incense Pa Brahim sells on the Jamaa al-Fna square in Marrakech, and it's in the bag!*

No? You're not interested? You're making a face. Too bad for you! I'll go peddle my idea to one of those bandits in Marrakech, you know, like that guy who managed to sell the neighborhood mosque to an American tourist by showing it to her between prayers, making her believe it was a *ryad*, so she took the bait, handed over a fat advance in dollars—not a check, oh no, wads of greenbacks.* When she came back six months later, she was so ashamed of having fallen for this scam that she burst out laughing with rage and left the city, saying Moroccans were the champions of cheating! The story made the rounds of Marrakech, to the crook's despair, because he had other projects in mind as juicy as the mosque deal. He'd already sold the same property a few times, a real cash cow, like that parking meter he'd installed downtown for a little steady income. One day he even managed to palm off one of his wife's caftans as an antique robe from the nineteenth century. He always manages to find suckers to swindle.

Mohammed laughed for a good long while, then forgot about his cousin and his fantastic schemes.

9

On September 5, 1962, when the chief administrator of the village, the *mokaddem*, dressed all in white, arrived at Mohammed's house to bring him his passport and inform him with solemn ceremony that in forty-eight hours he would set sail on his great journey, Mohammed found it hard to grasp how much time remained before he had to leave the village. The two men drank tea, ate a few honey crêpes, then took formal leave of each other as if that day were the most important one in Mohammed's life. He showed his wife the precious document: With this, I'll make you a queen and our son a prince! When she asked him the date of his departure, he stammered, Early in the morning. No one slept that night. The women prepared honey crêpes, some dried meat, figs, and dates. Mohammed and the other men who were leaving spent much of the evening in the baths, as if they were getting ready to be married or make a pilgrimage to Mecca. After the dawn prayer, they left the village on foot, then traveled in a rattletrap van to Marrakech, where they took a bus operated by the CTM, the state-run transportation company.

There were twenty men, some of whom came from neighboring villages. Time was passing so quickly now that Mohammed no longer gave it a thought. He had become light, agile, and indifferent to time, even though a faint fear of the unknown was peeking over the horizon. Actually, Mohammed had lost his bearings. A veteran was in charge of the group, an old hand at making this trip.

Remember this carefully, he told them: Wherever you go, whatever work you do, you can count on one thing, that Morocco will never let you go, will always be with you, impossible to forget, because Morocco is emigrating with you, following you, guiding and protecting you, sticking to your skin, so you must never get discouraged, never hesitate to talk to your compatriots when you feel homesick, and you'll see, it's very nice of LaFrance—I say Lalla França and *yes*, I *know* LaFrance is no princess or *sherifa*—to give us work and thus contentment. It's cold there, but it's cold back home in the winter too; over there, no friends, we'll always be off by ourselves together, because we're just guests, people invited in to do the hard work they don't do anymore, but us, we're strong, in good health, and we'll show them that a Berber doesn't fear cold or snow or fatigue because over there, you'll see, there's no time to be tired, and although you'll hear things from other old hands, don't listen to them; do your job and stick to that.

Lalla França pays well, but you mustn't think that on Sunday people will invite you home for dinner—that, no, never, because over there each person is in his house, the door is closed, the windows too, but that's how it is, period! That's the way they live: they'll never come bothering you, knocking on your door to ask for some salt or oil, no; that's not done. Everyone stays home and each to his own. There's not much hospitality over there, whereas hospitality is part of our way of life, one of our strengths, and sometimes we overdo it. Our houses are open to strangers—that's perfectly normal; it's our morality, our religion, which is why we have such trouble understanding why other people don't behave as we do.

You'll see, when you arrive you'll be lost. It's nothing like our countryside, nothing: climate, faces, landscapes, all different. You'd best get ready to enter a completely unknown world, as if you were in a dream in which we're no longer ourselves. Over there, you'll have free medicines and medical care, not like back home where there isn't even a nurse looking in on you from time to time—of course when I say "free," that means you cough up part of your paycheck every month, we all do, it's like we say back home: "Hand in hand and God's hand above all others." That's how the French understand solidarity, and if I weren't afraid of asking for trouble, I'd say they're almost Muslims.

And finally, remember: to avoid trouble, don't mess with politics, stay out of the way, and never intervene in a fight. Respect, respect. They lump Tunisians, Moroccans, and Algerians together, to them we're all Arabs, plus they don't distinguish between Arabs and Berbers, they know nothing about all that, so pay attention.* LaFrance will never be your country, that's for sure! LaFrance is LaFrance, a country that's rich but needs us just as we need it.

The train station was between the beach and the harbor, and children were crossing the tracks, making obscene gestures at the locomotives. Arriving in Tangier in the early morning, Mohammed felt ashamed to be discovering the sea so late in life—a calm sea of limpid blue, transformed into a living mirror by the first rays of the rising sun. Mohammed also felt delighted. No one had ever told him anything about the sea. He'd known that Agadir was a seaside town, but he'd never been there, and now he had time to walk on the sand and even taste salt water. He was twenty and had never dipped a finger into the sea. Behaving like a child, he played with the sand, dabbled in the water, splashed some on his face, in his hair. It was a lovely day. He bought a bottle of Coca from a passing vendor, drank it, then filled the bottle with seawater and took it with him, knowing he couldn't drink it, keeping it as a souvenir, to remind him of this particular day when he discovered the sea, the entire sea. When his companions made fun of him, he laughed. How could they understand, especially when some of them hailed from Casablanca or Bouznika, a little city right on the Atlantic coast?

The crossing was long and rough, thanks to an east wind that came up around noon. In the Spanish port of Algeciras, Mohammed was struck by the number of policemen. They were suspicious and aggressive, circulating among the passengers with muzzled dogs at their sides. Occasionally they demanded that certain suitcases be opened, and dumped the contents carelessly on the ground. Finding nothing, they'd simply walk away laughing, saying things in which the word *moros* cropped up often.* Mohammed found Spain not much more modern looking than Morocco.

The train trip was interminable: sometimes the locomotive sped up; sometimes it stopped dead because of work on the tracks. Mohammed tried in vain to sleep. Walking up and down the corridor, he watched the trees, fields, and houses streaming past. He thought about what their guide had said and prepared himself to live in a country where, no matter what happened, he would be alone. He couldn't digest the fact that he would not find the tribe waiting for him, the family, the native countryside that was a part of his body and whole being. He sensed that something was leaving him, that the farther the train went, the smaller his village shrank and would go on shrinking, until it disappeared. When he thought about his family, their image became blurred; he did not realize that he was passing from one time to another, one life to another. He was changing centuries, countries, customs. He felt as if his head were too small to deal with all that, and he paced like a caged animal. Too many new and unexpected things. Too many changes.

When the train stopped in the middle of some fields, he felt lost and thought back over his life, his small, orderly life, in which nothing special had happened. He'd seen his father and grandfather live that way, so it had been only natural for him to follow suit. He wasn't the first of his tribe to emigrate, however. Gripped with anguish, he understood that he was becoming an MWA, a Moroccan worker abroad. In time he would become an MRA, a Moroccan resident abroad. Where was the difference? "Resident" sounded better. But the way people looked at you was the same.

Mohammed still remembered precise images from his arrival in France: walls so gray they were almost black; impassive faces; a dense throng walking quickly, saying nothing; the strange smell of dust and stale perfume. People of color swept the streets and the corridors of the *métro*. There were rich people, and others apparently not as rich, but all of them had cars that looked almost new. Large advertisements displayed scantily clad women; others showed animals praising the quality of washing machines. Mohammed couldn't figure out what cats and dogs had to do with that. After stepping in some dog shit, he'd suddenly noticed that dogs were everywhere in this country. Why? Back home a dog was obviously an intruder, an animal to be driven away with stones. If a dog or cat walked in front of him while he was at prayer, he felt obliged to start all over again. To a Muslim, an animal is a carrier of dangerous germs, something to be avoided, and anyway there are no dogs in paradise. So this was Lalla França and its strange promise!

Time had engulfed these people, and he found their mystery unfathomable. Where were all these men and women going? Why in such a hurry? Where were their children? Why so many dogs? Why didn't they chat on the bus or in the *métro*? They ignored one another, read books or newspapers, but absolutely would not talk. He watched them and wondered if they noticed him. No, why would anyone pay attention to him? Was he special in any way? He looked at his face reflected in the window of the *métro* car and smiled faintly. At the Saint-Lazare stop a huge woman, an African in colorful clothing, got on with her healthy, laughing baby in a stroller. The child was happy and so was she. Paying no mind to anyone else, she took the boy onto her lap and began breast-feeding him. She was right at home. The other passengers looked on goggle-eyed. The firm and massive breast almost covered the infant's head! While the baby nursed, the mother talked to him as if she were alone under a tree back in her village. Mohammed envied her freedom. That woman was magnificent. Smiling and at ease. Mohammed began to grin. She looked up at him and said, Welcome to France!

How had she known he'd just arrived? It must have been obvious from his posture, from his worried expression. He helped her get the stroller off at her station and walked with her to the exit, where she thanked him with a pat on the back. She was strong; Mohammed was thrown off balance, and now he was lost too, without any idea where he was. He'd come out of the *métro* just to take a little look at the city, to begin making the country's acquaintance. He had to get back on the line going toward Gennevilliers, in the northwestern suburbs of Paris. He studied the *métro* map and felt even more confused. When a young man with long hair asked him where he wanted to go, Mohammed showed him a slip of paper with some words on it. He'd thought it was the name of a street, but it was a special housing project for immigrant workers, and on a weekday the place was almost deserted. A middle-aged man walking with a cane asked him grumpily, What are you doing in this country? Look at me: an accident at work, and no money. Go home, at least back there you'll be with your folks, your family, whereas here—no family, no wife, no mosque, nothing, work, work, and then the accident! A bad omen, thought Mohammed. The other man went on his way, balancing a big suitcase on one shoulder. A Frenchman showed Mohammed to his room; it was tiny, gloomy, with a low ceiling and walls so thin he could hear his neighbors breathing. The man said, Room 38. Here's the key, and remember: no women, no trouble, buy a lock or you'll get robbed. The toilet's over there, so's the shower. Okay, Mokhamad, welcome! Mohammed later learned that he called all the immigrants Mokhamad.

10

What Mohammed now had to do was get to his feet, put away the prayer rug, close up that crack in the wall, stop that gone-crazy clock, and announce to his wife that as of tomorrow he would begin his 'tirement: the end of his working life, a change of habits, a new existence. How could he tell her all that? He'd have to prepare her, find the right tone, simple words. If I sound happy, she'll be content; if I feel sorry for myself, she'll be disheartened. It was momentous news. He wasn't used to talking to her about his work. But what will I do with a new life? he wondered. I really liked the old one. I'd gotten quite used to it, had no gripes; I got up and left for the plant, it was work, that's all, yet I was fond of that routine, that early morning departure, with my lunch box in my bag. What will a new life be like? Colorful, full of joy? Or dull and cheerless? I didn't ask for anything. I'm not the type to ask for anything at all. In a pinch I might dare to ask for directions: Where is city hall please thank you very much excuse me for bothering you. . . .

According to his documents, he'd reached the mandatory age. Suddenly he remembered that he'd had to add on two extra years for some administrative reason known only to the *mokaddem* back home. Negotiate with management? Gain two more years of work at the plant? Scrounge around for whatever he could get, even offer to work for less pay, but above all, avoid winding up without any work, any routines. Why forbid a man in good health to work? It was too late now, though, to fiddle with his papers. He might even risk prosecution for having lied. He gave up his idea; he wasn't the kind to commit fraud. Said not a word to his wife or children.

As usual he rose early, made his ablutions, prayed, donned his overalls, fixed himself some tea that he drank standing up as if he were late, took the lunch box prepared by his wife, and left the apartment, saying, See you tonight. It was seven o'clock. On his way to the station, he stumbled two or three times. A small worry kept nagging at him: he should have been sleeping late that day, taking a bath, dressing as if for a holiday, beginning his new life. Something inside him was fighting back; he felt that his fate had strayed from the line traced long before, a clear, straight, dignified line. He took the *métro*, recognized some familiar faces, smiled a couple of times, then got off at his usual stop. He sat down on a bench to reflect. What exactly am

I doing? I must snap out of this. The plant is over. I can't handle the assembly line anymore. I'm ridiculous. People will make fun of me. I'll be a unique case in the history of this plant. No one's ever seen an employee return to work when he's been fortunate enough to retire! I'm not even looking to earn any money, I could just be there, be useful in case someone gets hurt or sick; I'd fill in for absentees, be the guy who keeps things going, get set up in an office where I'd wait for the call to go wherever I'm needed—and that's something that's never been done before. The unions would have a fit. They'd label me a troublemaker, say I was nuts. No, I don't want any problems with the unions, they don't like it when anyone steps out of line.

Outside the entrance to the plant, Marcel, the union delegate, came over to say how much he envied Mohammed in his retirement, having all his time to himself now. Mohammed smiled; he felt like offering to switch places with Marcel, but replied instead that he'd come to settle some administrative issues, that he was glad to have a chance to spend time with his children, whom he hadn't seen much of as they were growing up. He cranked out a few more empty phrases before thanking Marcel for his kindness. Standing at the big gate, he let the others pass by, stared for a while at the ground, took a last look at the entrance, now completely deserted, and walked away. Mohammed was despondent; he felt so sick at heart that his memory felt stuck in the day he'd arrived in France. He had trouble walking, felt his body collapsing, but he got a grip on himself and went to the nearest café to order a large glass of milk. Sitting at his table, he fiddled with the ashtray piled high with butts, then shoved it away and began to make plans.

He thought about spending a few months in Morocco, to start with, but he wouldn't act like Hassan, who'd taken advantage of his 'tirement to get himself a second wife—a younger, prettier one, obviously—and had never returned to France. He had promised the new wife to take her to the wonderland across the water, but his courage had failed him, and when his young wife became pregnant, Hassan was forced by the disapproval of his entire village to move to the city, where he wrote off his first family and his immigrant past, to start all over again in difficult conditions.

To Mohammed, abandoning your loved ones to begin a new life back home could only be the work of Satan, who loves to divide and destroy families. In his tribe that was not done, no: a man never deserted the mother of his children. Mohammed did not look at other women. He lowered his eyes whenever he spoke of his wife. He did not mention her name or pay her compliments or display any tenderness toward her—at least not in public. He barely glanced at his daughters, never said, How beautiful you are, my princess! Not like that character in a Lebanese soap opera he'd seen on TV.

Was he going to spend his days in Areski the Kabyle's café? To do what? Play cards or dominos? He didn't like either game.

Drink beer? Never. Watch TV, follow the races, daydream about those half-naked girls in the American shows? Didn't interest him. As Mohammed was leaving the café, one of his pals called out to him: It's my old friend! So, I hear you're in 'tirement, finally, free at last, can you imagine—they pay you not to work anymore, fantastic, no? That's France! So grateful to us, it's wonderful, not like back home, where if you get sick, you croak; if you go to the hospital, you have to buy your own medicines and even the thread they sew you up with after an operation, so if you're lucky, you make it, otherwise you're done for. Here, you see, you work, and, all right, we don't make millions, but we earn a good living, and then when you're tired out they give you your pension to live on, and you can still go to the hospital. It's free and first rate too, which is wonderful in this country where there's racism, as you know, but when you step into the hospital you're treated like everyone else, no racism— I can testify to that—and besides, when you go for a consultation, what do you see? There's more blacks and Arabs waiting than Frenchies, you ever notice? Not bad! No racism, plus you don't pay—*that's* LaFrance. This country—you've got to admit, after all—there's not just those Le Pen guys here. Hey, let's drink to that, I'll buy you a sparkling water! Me—thanks be to God and Mecca—I don't touch alcohol anymore, but cigarettes, ah, that's harder, I can't manage that, so anyway, what are you going to do with yourself? Move back home, take a pretty girl as a second wife—you're allowed, mind you, you can do as you please, and you know, Ammar is over sixty and he's a father again, got himself a girl and got her in the family way; it's all legal, but his kids won't have anything more to do with him, which is tough but his own fault, he should have been more discreet about it and above all, not made her pregnant! Well, so long, see you soon. Oh, I forgot to tell you: I opened a little grocery store nearby, I sell everything, stop by to see me sometime!

Mohammed remembered how Ammar's wife Rahma had taken revenge on him after he abandoned her for that brunette from Agadir. Arriving one day out of the blue with her five children, Rahma passed herself off as his younger sister, moved into the newlyweds' apartment, and presented the young wife with a fait accompli. Frightened, the girl ran home to her parents, who demanded a divorce and damages from the husband; seems he'd forgotten to mention that he was already married. The affair made a huge splash: the polygamous husband had to accept all Rahma's conditions, and once she was back in France (after beating him soundly without leaving any marks), Rahma demanded her own divorce—on the grounds of polygamy! Ammar had been ordered to pay three-quarters of his pension to his wife and children.

Rahma: now there was a strong, capable, determined woman. When the couple were Mohammed's neighbors, people used to say she beat her husband, but it was hard to believe, since in their milieu it was usually the other way round, and

Ammar wasn't the kind to complain and admit to any mistreatment by his wife. Although his pals suspected something, they didn't dare broach the subject with him, but they could see he was unhappy, listless, in poor shape. Rahma was the one who handled everything; Ammar came home from the factory, ate, and wasn't allowed to spend the family's money in bars. She always took charge of his earnings, letting him have only enough to go to the café now and then. Whenever he dared protest, she'd shut herself up with him in their bedroom and whack him with the children's big Larousse dictionary, and she must have had to buy them a new one, because the first one was a wreck. Physically she was stronger than Ammar, a peasant woman unfazed by anything, fearless, sure of herself, forging ahead, sweeping everything from her path. Ammar had thought about a divorce, but it was complicated, and besides, it just wasn't done in his tribe—Rahma was a distant cousin. No one would have believed him if he'd admitted she beat him, so he kept quiet, submitted, and like all weaklings, ran away instead of standing his ground. He'd thought to get back at her by leaving some money on the kitchen table and taking off, never imagining she would follow him to foil his plan.

Smiling at the idea of the henpecked husband, Mohammed began to walk along, staring idly at the sidewalk, with his fists clenched in his pockets, as if following a doctor's orders to get some exercise. When he thought about his children, he had the feeling he'd lost them. It was more than a feeling: a certainty, a definite certainty. It was as if he'd been pitched into a void, tipped into nothingness like a sack of trash. A sack full of useless junk. There was a dead rat in the sack, rotting away with a dreadful stench. I'm the sack and the rat, Mohammed told himself. I'm the rubble and the rusting iron. I'm the animal no one loves. He saw himself tossed onto a garbage dump, tumbling down its side with broken bits of things, old wires, debris, dust, and suddenly—oblivion. He no longer exists. No one thinks of him or wants to see him. He's at the end of the long road: it's over. None of his children has come to reclaim him from the dump. Then the rat woke up and scratched Mohammed's leg, making him jump: it was a plant he'd just brushed by.

II

Mohammed's son Mourad had a good position in a department store and had married Maria, a Spanish woman, born like him in France but whose parents had gone back home to Seville. Mourad was athletic. He could have been a professional soccer player, but he had a heart murmur, so he'd studied accounting and continued to play several sports. His greatest desire: to escape his suburban neighborhood and everyone in it to go live in Paris. He was fond of his parents but loved his freedom more, the independence he'd won by working even while he was still in school. He kissed his father's hand and his mother's forehead, signs of respect but not submission. As soon as he had begun earning money, Mourad had decided to give some of it to his parents, for which his father had thanked him, saying that the money would go toward the construction of the house. What house? Mohammed had only gestured vaguely and turned away without another word.

After his marriage, Mourad had stopped spending his vacation back in the village, preferring his in-laws' house in the mountains of the Alpujarras. He'd often wondered why the Spanish were more successful than Moroccans, and his wife had come up with an answer that shocked him: it was because of religion, because of Islam! Outraged, Mourad reacted as if he were an imam—although he himself never observed a single Muslim ritual. When Maria tried to clarify what she meant and described how Francoism had used the Catholic Church to cling to power, Mourad was hurt. Islam could not be a force for backwardness! Maria carefully explained that no religion on earth encouraged change and modernity, but Mourad had actually been thinking about his father, for whom Islam was more than a religion: it was a code of ethics, a culture, an identity. What would my father be without Islam? Mourad wondered. A lost man. He finds religion soothing. He loves his rituals; they bring him a peaceful sense of well-being.

One day Mourad's father-in-law took him to visit the palace and gardens of the Alhambra in Granada, where the young man was fascinated by the beauty of Arab architecture. It was your ancestors, said his father-in-law, who built these magnificent things. That was a long, long time ago. What a lovely civilization, and there's nothing left of it. Luckily, we're here to preserve these treasures.

Mourad was offended, yet unable to contradict his father-in-law. Facts were facts. What could he possibly say?

Mohammed no longer saw his eldest girl, Jamila, who had defied her parents and married an Italian. So painful had it been for him to see a non-Muslim enter the family that he'd behaved as if she were no longer his daughter. At first he'd tried to reason with her, but Jamila was in love, refused to discuss anything, and had tantrums the like of which he'd never seen before. It's my life, not yours! You're not going to keep me from living simply because we're Muslims! And just what kind of a religion is it that lets men marry Christian or Jewish women but won't let its women do the same with men? Well? You think I'll be happier with some countrified jerk, one of those lousy peasants who'll lock me up while he goes out to get drunk with his pals? No thanks, Papa, wake up: I decide how to live my life, so you can give me your blessing if you want, and if you don't approve, there's nothing I can do about such garbage! You're sick—you need to get help!

Mohammed had bowed his head and walked away with tears in his eyes. Trying to comfort him, his wife told him it would all blow over, and Jamila would soon come back home. Mohammed kept repeating, almost in a daze, But what's this being in love? What is this thing that's collapsing on me like a ruined house and breaking my back? Were we, you and I, in love? I don't know what that means, and you know how hard it is for me to talk about those things. Love: we don't discuss that; we see it at the movies, not in real life. Being in love! It means she's gone. She has fallen to the ground. It's like that business with Fatiha, who suddenly fell in with a man and never again set foot in the village, a man from the city, with money, and she left with him even though she knew he was married with five children. No, if my daughter follows this stranger of hers, she's not coming back to us again—it's over, it's him or us, it's him or her father. I don't want to see her anymore; she's no longer my daughter. I'll erase her from the family register, it's finished. A daughter I spoiled, giving her everything she wanted, brings to my house a Christian who never goes to the barber and who asks for my blessing? It's impossible, out of the question. I'll do what Louardi did: he refused to sanction the marriage of his daughter to a non-Muslim and he was right—a year later she came home: It's not working—we're different, too different.

When Mohammed's wife reminded him that Mourad had married a Christian woman, he shouted angrily, But he's a man, the man runs the family, and that Christian woman will convert to our religion in the end. No Christian man has ever sincerely converted to Islam to marry a Muslim woman! They pretend, change their name, recite the *shahada* to profess their new faith—and think no more about it.* No: it's the man who decides, not the woman.

Ever since Jamila had left the house, no one had spoken her name in Mohammed's presence. She had wounded him so deeply that he could not forget his pain.

On Eid al-Kebir, the Feast of the Sheep, Mohammed learned that his other two sons had dropped out of high school to go work in the provinces. None of his children were home for this all-important holiday except little Rekya and Nabile, and for the first time Mohammed realized that the boys had made lives for themselves elsewhere without anyone telling him. One son was a mechanic at a garage in Dreux; the other, who had a real nose for business, had gone to work in his uncle's grocery store in Compiègne, and he too sent his mother a money order from time to time. The apartment was now too big for Mohammed, his wife, Nabile, and Rekya, the last girl, who worked hard in school and wanted to be a veterinarian. The family had broken up.

Mohammed consoled himself with the thought that life was like that: You have children, you spoil them, then one day—off they go. They hardly remember us anymore, but what can you do? If we were in the village, they'd all be there, before my eyes, but here we're in a country that knows no pity: you must fight every moment to live, to breathe, to sleep in peace. Mohammed dreamed of bringing everyone back together and having a celebration, but since he was sure his children wouldn't come, he decided to fall ill, gravely ill. That was the solution! They would come to say good-bye to him in his hospital bed. Mohammed was superstitious, though: one shouldn't trifle with disease and death and the will of God. Now all his affection was turned toward Rekya, who, having neither the time nor the inclination to comfort him, shut herself in her room to study. At least she'll pass her finals, her father thought, and go on to graduate school. She'll be an animal doctor and will come give me a hand on the farm back home.

Mohammed couldn't imagine, still less accept, that his children's lives could slip through his hands. He would never forget what Jamila had shouted in anger: You're sick—you need to get help! Loving your children, wanting them to love you, wanting to be close to them and wishing only the best for them—that's being sick? That's why I need help? Fine: I'll go see a doctor for crazy people and tell him, Well, I'm sick because I love my children, so what medicine should I take for that? Should I swallow some anti-paternal-affection syrup or stuff myself with suppositories to make me forget I have five children, including a daughter who went off with someone foreign to our culture, our religion, and our land? Her behavior was appalling! And I—I did everything to raise my kids properly, I don't know where they got this raging resentment of their parents. I don't think French schools teach children to hate their mothers and fathers. No, it isn't school; it's the TV, all those American and French films where families aren't families anymore, where parents have lost their authority. And I need to get help! I'm sick, all right, and that's the way I like it!

One day their mother told me: A father should have authority or else nothing works. Just what is this *authority*? Is it the authority of fear? Is it being harsh, like those who beat their children only to lose them because they run away, get into drugs, and wind up in prison or the hospital morgue? I always thought that authority came naturally, that I had no need to shout or say the same thing over and over, but when children don't listen to you, when they do only as they please, then you're helpless. That's how it is, so you can only wait it out and hope they'll be smart enough not to get in trouble. My children have never torched a car or trashed any motorcycles. When the projects blow up, my kids are the first to be frightened by what their friends get up to. They always wanted to be successful, were never tempted by violence and disorder.

It was Nabile who came to console him. He took Mohammed's hand, embraced him, and they looked into each other's eyes. Then they went out to a café to have some ice cream.

That afternoon, his head heavy with sorrow, Mohammed hugged Nabile tight without saying a word, blinking back tears. He waited for Rekya to get home from school, kissed her, packed his suitcase, prepared a few provisions, and told his wife, I'm going back home to rest for a while. You'll come join me with Nabile and Rekya over vacation, so, I'll leave you some money, and if you need anything, go see Sallam.

Mohammed was going to take the train, since his car—along with many others—had been torched that October, when some youths had gone on a rampage after the accidental electrocution of two of their friends.* The 78—the post office code for Yvelines—had not erupted, but some kids eager to play copycat had set fire to cars in the neighborhood just for the hell of it, to impress everyone, make a statement. What were they trying to say by burning my Renault? thought Mohammed sadly. Bought on credit at a good price because I was an employee of the firm. . . . What did I ever do to those wretched kids? Why did they take away my car, when I'm on their side, when we're of the same blood? Who knows! Someone forgot to bring them up right. Great: those kids, lowlifes, raised rotten, lousy students, disobedient to their parents, couldn't find anything better to do than set fire to my old car that was so useful to me, especially in the summer. And the insurance guy told me to forget it. Without even looking up at me he says, We are not liable. Those are risks we don't insure: bad weather, natural catastrophes, civil disorder on public thoroughfares—that's not our responsibility. We insure against accidents, not gang rebellions, and anyway, if that's the case, it's one of your kids who set the fire, because my son isn't going to torch my car, you follow me? So I can't help you. Forget your car, buy another one, but if I were you I'd wait for things to calm down. They adore new cars, such a temptation. . . . Au revoir, monsieur, so sorry, really.

Mohammed had left the insurance office in despair. Why didn't the French state reimburse poor people victimized by these disturbances? He looked around him; there were almost no parked cars: people had taken precautions. Mohammed just couldn't understand how young people he saw every day in the elevator would abruptly try to set the city on fire because they were bored, because they wanted to stick it to LaFrance. But I'm not LaFrance! I'm a simple family man stranded in the street without a car to drive back home, that's all. I've never shouted at those kids hanging out in the neighborhood, and my children didn't have anything to do with them, I'm sure of that, because they went to work at an early age and don't live here anymore.

What should I do now? File a complaint at the police station? No, they won't listen to me, and they're swamped in any case and too angry. Never talk to an angry policeman. Besides, I hate going into a police station. I'll take the train, then the boat, then the bus, then a taxi. It will take a long time, I'd better travel light—I'll have to repack my luggage. Or I could wait until Thursday to take the Gennevilliers–Agadir bus. Yes, but last year the driver fell asleep: twenty dead and as many injured. Can't trust it. Run by Moroccans who want to make a lot of money in a hurry, so they hire drivers they pay poorly and give them a small bonus only if they drive fast and get there first. So, the driver in the accident got a big bonus: death, poor fellow! The government ought to do something about those buses, but the companies are all corrupt, they pay for whatever they want—permits, surcharges, speeding. Too bad, I'll take the train, at least I'll be able to sleep. Well, maybe not, but I'll try.

12

For the first time in his life abroad, Mohammed did not drive on and on (as he had put it) to get back home. He had already forgotten his ruined car and bought his train ticket but was in no hurry. Retirement meant time he now needed to occupy, to fill with projects. He spent all night planning how he could finally gather his entire little family back around him. Although tempted to curse Lalla França for stealing his children, he pulled himself together and asked God to return things to normal. And for him, normal meant that the children would stay home, even when married; that they should come visit him often in the village; and that they should make plans together. For instance, what if they all went to Mecca as a family? Mohammed daydreamed about this expensive trip, imagining everyone going around the Kaaba and praying. Folly? Madness? Not at all: the duty of every Muslim. But he was not in a

Muslim country. He had to abandon such ideas and find more viable projects. Open a grocery store? No, wouldn't work. Why not offer his family a complete tour of Morocco, from north to south, like those French families who visit the country by stopping everywhere, staying with the locals, eating in little restaurants, and having a ball? He'd buy a small van, and they'd go off on an adventure! Since his children all worked and couldn't schedule their vacations on the same dates, he'd do the trip two or three times, showing off the country, meeting its people, admiring its beauty and wonderfully varied landscapes. The travelers would talk to one another, camp out, invent games, spend many happy hours together. Why didn't I do that when the children were little? I never thought of it. I followed the same ritual every year from July 15 to August 28, doing the same things. That was our destiny. We had to accept that, without any questions. I don't know of a single emigrant who has toured Morocco with his family. We'd leave the 78 and head for the village, a place without a number, in the back of beyond.

He would tackle the construction of the house as soon as he returned to the village, in that flat, arid, pitiless countryside without a trace of green. No tree had ever survived out there; no vegetation had ever managed to thrive. All along the road were thistles, thorn bushes, gray shrubs with stalks like slender knives, and big stones, yellow dust, flies—flies everywhere, especially on days when a sheep's throat was cut. When it's hot, people go to ground in their homes until dusk, learning to wait, learning to do nothing. They don't talk about the climate and its hardships. They sit cross-legged on mats, shifting positions, then changing places. They don't even look at the sky. They cover the well, afraid that the water will evaporate, and they forget about the hours that drag by. Instead of passing from one person to another, words seem to bump into the walls and crumble away. So no one speaks. There's nothing to say, nothing to do. Perhaps folks following the progress of a line of busy ants will watch a few stragglers tumble into crevices, and let them die. Such harshness hardens hearts. Codes of behavior are cold and rigid. A disobedient child gets slapped silly. A girl who looks too noticeably at a man is shut away. No argument, no negotiation. Life is simple, and simply terrible. A tiny window onto the outside world came only with the first butane-gas-powered television sets, but people laughed as they watched them, seeing an exotic world even more savage than their own flicker into the village on the black-and-white screens. Everyone watched films, and whenever a man and woman held hands, our women would veil their faces, some of them exclaiming, These Christians have no shame! No modesty at all. We're better off here at home. But what do our men get up to in those countries? Do they let these scrawny shadows seduce them into vice? Do they squander their money on these loose women?

———

Begun five years earlier, work on the house had stopped for lack of money. Now that Mohammed was determined to finish it, his life in retirement had meaning. He no longer saw time as a terrifying specter: time had expanded, grown light, colorful, airy; he imagined it as a kite on a soft breeze in a clear sky. Time had let go of him, allowing him a second chance. Perhaps he had failed somehow in France, but time was letting him pursue a different success in Morocco.

Mohammed envisioned a big, handsome house, full of light and children; he'd never been bothered by the shouts and rambunctious antics of youngsters. He smiled. He drew the house in his head, left enough space for the flower garden, counted the trees to be planted, reviewed the varieties of roses to be ordered at the market in Marrakech, and organized the kitchen garden, which he decided to entrust to Nabile, who would certainly take good care of it.

Tears welled in his eyes as he thought of the boy, but he blinked them away. Nabile had a winning personality, lots of imagination, and he made Mohammed laugh, helping him forget his conflicts with the other children. Mohammed saw him as a prince in the new house, a prince and a leader. Nabile was the only one he could count on. The boy liked to be trusted, to be given things to do. He had always wanted to grow up, to be an adult at an early age and leave behind the childhood he associated with his own backwardness. By growing up, Nabile thought he would become like everyone else. He used to say, Me mgolian? Head's mess up? Me sixteen, champion, fishing! So, Grampa, we go?

The closer Mohammed came to the Moroccan frontier, the larger the house became, the taller the walls rose, the bigger the bedrooms grew, while the ivy climbed faster, plants swayed, birds sang. Mohammed could even hear the soft sound of the fountain he would install in the courtyard. It wasn't a house anymore; it was a corner of paradise, a kind of palace with gardens, parks, animals of all kinds. A tale from *One Thousand and One Nights*. A huge carpet woven by hundreds of hands. All that was missing was Harun al-Rashid and his court. Nabile would play his role perfectly, since he adored acting and conjuring tricks.

All alone, Mohammed was dreaming and laughing, seeing himself dressed in white, welcoming the authorities arriving to inaugurate the ideal house built by the model emigrant, who had always sent part of his salary home to Morocco, who had invested in his country and intended to repatriate his entire family. On the day celebrating the Feast of the Throne, commemorating the accession of His Majesty King Mohammed VI, the king would bestow a decoration on the model emigrant, who would appear before him in his gray suit (slightly rumpled), a brand-new white shirt, and a flowered tie. Placing a hand on his shoulder, the king would walk a few paces with him in front of the television cameras, filling Mohammed with such pride that his problems would melt away, and the sovereign would send a special plane to bring his children and their mother back to Morocco.

Mohammed saw himself as tall, slender, his pockets stuffed with money for him to distribute to the needy. He was wild with joy. He envisioned himself running through fields, leaping in delight like a carefree child. That's what it was to please oneself, to arrange things so that life now offered him a superb gift. He had always felt that God had been lenient with him by making him a good father and husband. None of his children had ever been involved with the police, and he thought of poor Larbi, whose eldest son was in prison for armed assault, while the youngest boy suffered from that disease Mohammed was too superstitious to mention. Mohammed considered himself lucky. He thought of his youngest daughter and was determined that she should study veterinary medicine.

Someone at the auto plant, an activist who strongly opposed the politics of the French state, had explained to him why almost no sons of immigrants attended French universities: You see, our children aren't dumber than others; it's that they're discouraged from primary school on, quickly channeled into technical schools. And I'm not saying that's bad, but why can't our children go to the competitive state-run universities, you know, the ones where they wear uniforms as though they were in the army? Why aren't they in banking, doing research, involved in the big doings of this fucking country? I'm not talk-ing about our friends on the left who've done zip; I mean, in Holland and Belgium there are deputies—yes, deputies!—with roots in the Maghreb, and there's even a young woman of Moroccan background who's a minister of culture in Brussels, while here, in France, we have the right to fill up the prisons, wait around in police stations, and be harassed as soon as we speak up. That's what disgusts me, and our generation. We're done for, but why should our sons suffer the same fate? You know what? It's the old colonial reflex: doesn't matter how per-fect you are; you've always got to jump higher and farther than their champions, that's how it is, that's our lot. So the kids get scared, pissed off, feel lost. They try to set everything on fire. They burned my jalopy, and the insurance people told me "no coverage," "exceptional circumstances," "kiss your car good-bye." And the kids don't go to ritzy Neuilly to put on their act, no, they burn *their* schools, *our* buses, *our* cars, they hurt themselves—then get labeled evil immigrants. And do you think my son's an immigrant? He's never left the 78. He's a Frenchy, 100 percent.

13

When the train stopped in the middle of the countryside, putting an end to his dream, Mohammed stood up to stretch his legs and looked out at the sky. The moon shone so intensely that some of the shooting stars seemed, in its brilliant whiteness, like drops of water from a summer rain shower. Mohammed began to pray, to thank God for having helped him escape 'tirement by giving him a good idea to keep him busy. He felt proud and, above all, impatient. Time was flying by; he had to get to the village quickly and immediately call the master mason, Bouazza, to set him building again. When the train began to move once more, Mohammed sank into a contented drowsiness in which he saw himself surrounded by all his dear ones as the seasons rolled by. He gave a color to each season: white for summer, a grayish blue for autumn, luminous green for winter, golden yellow for spring. He liked painting time with colors. Now that he'd left France, the colors had come back. And music, too.

When Mohammed disembarked at Tangier, he had to wait a while for the afternoon bus to Casablanca. Leaving his suitcase in a locker, he took a walk along the sandy coast road. Everything had changed since his first discovery of the sea. Young men were playing soccer or loitering nearby; a few beggars stopped him, and he gave them some coins. Around him he saw more and more buildings under construction. Mohammed sat down at a café and was approached by a salesman: You want to buy an apartment in one of these fine buildings? Ten thousand dirhams a square meter! It's a good buy: you choose from the blueprint, then move in a year later with everything—running water, electricity, television, telephone, and even the Internet, everything! You give me a down payment, I give you a receipt, and next year we meet again in this café, right here at this table. Is it a deal? No, thanks.

In the meantime, at least ten beggars had passed by with their hands out: women with babies, cripples, healthy young people, elderly folks showing him crumpled old drug prescriptions. There are more and more of them, Mohammed thought. This country has lost its pride—it's overwhelming, there are too many beggars, too much corruption and injustice, and the longer it goes on, the more it becomes too much.

Thinking about the journey still ahead of him, Mohammed figured he would arrive home at last in a day and a half, thirty-six hours if all went well: Tangier to Casa, wait; Casa to Agadir, wait; Agadir to home in a taxi. Wait, wait, patience, patience! That's what he'd been told in Mecca: *As-sabr ya Hajj!* Patience, Hajji! The magic formula. He had learned patience during the pilgrimage but had lost it over time, becoming anxious and trying hard to hide it. Now Mohammed felt a tiny flame of anger flare up in him again: Why did they burn my car? Why didn't the insurance company give me anything, not even enough to rent another one while the government found a way to help those thousands of people who lost their cars, which they often needed for their jobs? Then Mohammed remembered that he hadn't had the presence of mind to correct the insurance guy when the fellow had put the blame on immigrants. Those youngsters who torched cars and set public buildings on fire are not immigrants! They're probably—maybe definitely—the children of immigrants, but *they aren't immigrants!* Even the TV had talked about immigration. There was nothing normal, nothing fair about all this. The only thing Mohammed knew for sure was that he'd had nothing to do with it, and neither had his children.

Bouazza, the master mason, had moved to Marrakech and was busy with several building sites at the same time. He had grown rich and hard to get hold of, having evidently forgotten where he came from. Once he reached home, Mohammed forgot about Bouazza and called upon his many nephews and cousins, who set to work. He recovered the energy of his youthful days, and his worries were erased by concrete and whitewash. Neighbors came to see this strange, shapeless building so unlike their own homes, and after asking a few questions, they went away wondering if Mohammed had lost his mind. He was definitely losing weight, sleeping next to the building materials, not taking care of himself. He had paid an architect to draw up plans, but instead of using them the mason was following the instructions of Mohammed, who wasn't managing to explain very well what it was he wanted.

He kept saying, I want a big house, bigger than all the poky houses in the village, a house as big as my heart. People should be able to see it from far away and say that's where Mohammed lives with his whole family—I mean, with all his children. Yes, my children will come live with me here, in these infinite spaces. My children and grandchildren. It will be the house of happiness, of harmony and peace!

Mohammed would fall silent, wondering if he'd gone too far. He had become unrecognizable, while the house had lost all sense of proportion, all logic, except, perhaps, that of Mohammed's obsession: to reunite the entire family beneath this roof resembling the lid of a giant cooking pot in which nothing was in its right place.

———

After five months, the house was almost ready, although it still needed painting, shutters, windows, and all those details that make a place habitable. To keep it a surprise, Mohammed hadn't told any of his children about the house. Actually, he'd been afraid they might discourage him, since they were used to speaking their minds and would have wounded him with their words, so he didn't want to know what they thought, preferring to astonish them.

His wife had rejoined him, and she knew that her husband was making a mistake, feeding on illusions, but she kept quiet, as usual. She had realized long ago that her sons and daughters did not belong to them anymore: the children loved their lives and felt neither remorse nor regret. They had been whisked away by the whirlwind of France, and she had watched them go, knowing that she had no way to hold them back, to keep them close to her and her husband. She'd looked around and seen that, in one way or another, France swallowed up the children of foreigners. Actually, the reality was simpler: there was no plot, no trap, no aggressive wish to rob immigrants of their children, but it was only natural for kids to love their native land, and Mohammed's wife knew she stood no chance against such an attachment. She did try to talk to her children, advise them, warn them to be careful, but they barely listened. The streets swept them away into adventure, toward new people and things and a life quite different from that of their parents: the auto plant, shift work, sadness and fatigue, the five or six weeks back in the village, the routines and cramped space of that life—none of it was really worth keeping, so they'd kept almost none of it. Find your own luck, choose your own fate.

But you don't think about that if you're a parent, you just get on with life, and then one day you realize the damage has been done. Fell off the truck! That was their mother's favorite expression. She'd learned it by heart without knowing exactly what it meant. To her, it evoked the tiny accidents, the wounds of life, as if the family had been riding on a truck with a tendency to skid. Problems? Fell off the truck! And Mohammed, all the while, had been dreaming of building the biggest house in the village, just as in the old days. Forty years in France hadn't changed him. Not one whit. He remained intact, inviolable, impeccable: naturally and hermetically sealed. Nothing of France had found a place in his heart or his soul. It hadn't even been a conscious, deliberate decision. He was what he was; nothing could change him. There were millions like him. They emigrated as if encased in armor, fiercely resisting all outside influence: we have our lives, our ways, and they have theirs. Each to his own—no intrusion, no meddling. Mohammed never even lifted a finger to defend himself against what he called the contamination of LaFrance, for he was foreign, utterly unreachable. The village and its traditions back home lived on in him, coming between him and reality. He was in his world, where he lived without much introspection. His touchstone for everything was Islam: My religion is my identity. I am a Muslim before being a Moroccan, before becoming an immigrant. My refuge is Islam, which calms me and brings me peace; it is the last revealed religion, destined to close a lengthy chapter that God began a long, long time ago. Here they have their faith, and we have ours. We are not made for them or they for us. The contract is clear: I work, they pay me, I raise my children, and then one day we all go home to our house, yes, because the house is my country, my native land.

When his wife had first set eyes on the huge house, she'd let out a loud whinny of surprise, and then, thinking he might turn it into an amusement park for the children when they came on vacation, she asked him what he was planning to do with it. Live in it, he'd answered. You, me, and all our children. It's simple: this house is our star, our most precious treasure, since each stone is a drop of my blood, every wall a slice of my life, and we will finally be reunited to live as before, as I lived, as my father lived, for I am only following the path laid out by those who came before us and who know better than we do what is good for our offspring. I've provided for everything: everyone has a bedroom with a bathroom, wardrobes for storing winter clothes, and I've bought a giant television for the patio, where together we'll watch entertaining shows, you'll see, plus I've built a hammam and a prayer room, so this will be the house of happiness, and I'm even thinking of installing an intercom, like the one we have in the building in LaFrance, because it would be nice to ring the children in their rooms before going there, and I've also planned—right next door—a poultry yard with the best roosters and hens, and although there won't be any rabbits because I know you don't like them, there will be other animals: ewes, lambs, one or two cows. So no more reason to go to the supermarket—that's nice, right? I'm very pleased. And you, you're pleased, I've done well, don't you think? I've sunk almost all my savings into this and even borrowed a bit. Stone, land, they're solid, much better than money. Look around you: no one has a house as grand and beautiful as this. I've succeeded, yes, I've made a success of it—proof that a man can go abroad and return to his village unchanged; it's wonderful. Me, I figured it all out: to work and save money we needed LaFrance, but LaFrance is good for the French, not for us. We don't belong over there. They have their religion, they marry and divorce like anything, but then there's us, who have our religion, and when we marry, it's for life, for always. So you understand: I'm going to save our children, I'll rescue them from the other religion, bring them back to us to keep living the life our parents and grandparents did, because the solution is definitely nowhere else but here, where there is plenty of space, and besides, here the earth is good. See how those plants have grown. The drought is over; there's no reason for our children to live far away from us. No, no reason. . . . He kept saying that, with a strange gleam in his eyes. He was possessed, haunted by an obsession, repeating words endlessly, talking to himself, scratching his head, stopping only to gaze at the sky and talk to the rare clouds drifting by.

Afraid of shattering his hopeful enthusiasm, his wife said nothing. She had nothing to say. As usual. She was not supposed to contradict her husband: that was their pact. Perhaps he was loosing his wits, but how could she help him, bring him back to reason? She didn't know. She placed her problem in the hands of God, because she knew that he never abandons those who worship and pray to him.

14

The house was bizarre. It looked like an overloaded truck or a poorly tied-up package. It was a blot on the landscape. Tilting to one side, it seemed about to fall and crush Mohammed, whose disorganized instructions had been closely followed by the mason. Right, he'd say. Here we need a nice, big room for my oldest son and his wife. She's a foreigner and I'd like to please them, show them that even though we're poor we have large hearts, so the bedroom must be as big as my heart, you understand; then next door we need more rooms, everyone gets one, and don't forget the hammam, the oven, a place for the hens and the sheep because, you see, the house should be like a little palace, a poor man's palace but handsome, welcoming, spacious, magnificent, so go to it, draw, do your work, and don't forget the windows and the fans for summer, since the children come mostly in the summer. See if you can make me a small swimming pool—I know, there's no water, but by the time you finish building it the water will be here.

What a house! A mistake, a folly. The balconies were narrow, the windows tiny, and the front door immense. In the middle was a courtyard, a sort of Andalusian patio, where Mohammed had planted a shrub doomed to certain demise in that arid climate. The floor was of the finest quality concrete but still waiting for the *zelliges*, glazed mosaic tiles that had been ordered from Fez, or at least that's what the mason claimed. The walls were of *tadelakt*, a gleaming, moisture-resistant plaster, and some of them were whitewashed. From the ceiling hung electric wires without bulbs; electricity was one of the village *caïd*'s promises. The bathrooms were fully equipped, but running water was another of those promises. That said, no one importuned the *caïd* for anything anymore, knowing that results did not depend on him and, in any case, everything came from Rabat.

But who could he be, this improbable character off somewhere in an air-conditioned office, who one morning would entertain a tiny thought for the inhabitants of this hardscrabble village, and who then might actually help out Mohammed in his quest to remedy the absurd injustices of a life in exile? Best not to think about that! The image of that petty bureaucrat in Rabat bedeviled Mohammed. He imagined him, saw him, smelled him. He wears a dark brown suit, a gray shirt he hasn't changed in four days, a black tie. He raises an arm

occasionally to sniff his armpit. He perspires and has no de-
odorant to dispel the odor of accumulated sweat. Once he
tried a bottle of perfume bought from a specialist in fake luxury
goods; it gave him an itchy rash of pimples. This bureaucrat
smokes and complains constantly about his meager salary. Less
gifted than his colleagues, who have managed to build up nice
little nest eggs by selling promises here and there, he doesn't
know how to lie and is unfamiliar with the tricks of his trade,
for making money on the side in the Ministry of Public Works.
This gives ammunition to his wife, who wages domestic guer-
rilla war on him every day. So how do you expect this man, a
decent sort on the whole, to consider the problems of a thousand peasants who've acquired the habit of living without
water or electricity? He thinks instead about earning himself
a little money and his wife's respect, which are more important than the house of Mohammed Thimmigrant.

The petty bureaucrat scratches his head, rubs his hand
over his greasy hair, picks at a pimple, opens a file, flips through
the pages, pretends to search for a word, looks up, notices a
spiderweb in a corner of the ceiling, looks down, resigned, then
underlines Mohammed's request with a red pen. He wants
potable water! And why not enough to fill a swimming pool!
Water! Do I demand champagne when I get home? These
peasants who don't realize that the state can do nothing for
them—they emigrate, make a pile of money, and arrogantly
demand water and electricity from us as if they lived in the city!

Since time immemorial the country people have lived with well water and used candles for light, a bottled-gas generator to run the TV, and just because they've lived in Europe doesn't mean they have the right to pester us. I mean, I'm willing to make an effort, but they don't understand that they must contribute to the expense. I'd like to emigrate too. My wife would be delighted; she could even consult some fancy doctors and finally have children. She says it's my fault—I had to knock up the maid to get her to give up that argument. Luckily, the maid had a miscarriage, and my wife fired her after a detailed interrogation. Well, that's another story. I'm assigning this dossier to the "on hold" pile, which will soon be five years old! It's part of the furniture, the landscape; I can't imagine this office without that pile.

What can I do to make my wife be nice to me? Give her a present? But it would have to be something special: the keys to a new car, the deed to some property, or at least a gold necklace or a diamond ring, a trip to Turkey, maybe camping out by the pyramids under a starry night sky—or, better yet, a briefcase full of money. Ever since she saw that in an Egyptian film, she's been dreaming of it.

Watch how the other men get on, she keeps telling me, the real men, not limp noodles like you! Study them, at least try to learn from them, and don't come near me, don't try to cry on my shoulder, because in that movie it's only after handing over the little briefcase full of money that the husband took the liberty of resting his head on his wife's shoulder. Don't count on me to wash your hair. Leave it greasy with dirt; that's you in a nutshell. My husband—or shall I say my alleged husband?—has greasy hair because his pockets are empty, because he can't satisfy his wife either sexually or financially. His wife is frustrated! She would willingly have gone off with someone else, but she has principles.

The petty bureaucrat begins to count the number of files on hold. Two hundred fifty-two files. Not one has a chance of getting anywhere. He scratches his head, looks at his fingernails clogged with dandruff. Turning toward a colleague, he suggests they go out for a coffee.

15

The day Mohammed moves in, the house is not completely finished, but nothing stops him. He's obstinate—that's built into him, part of his character. There's an expression, "stubborn as a mule," but a mule can't hold a candle to Mohammed and his tribe. He refuses to face facts, forges ahead as if permanently locked on to rails. Doesn't talk things over (forget that!), plunges in headfirst and eyes closed, convinced he's absolutely right. Hardheaded, headstrong, strong willed. Impregnably and single-mindedly devoted to the idée fixe, inflexible to the end. No, a stubborn man is a nut impossible to crack because he clings with everything he's got to what is primitive and archaic. Mohammed doesn't know it, but his obstinacy is at the core of his being.

In his house there is a room for every child, but they all have different dimensions. Some connect to each other through a low, awkward door. The small windows are of various sizes. The prayer room takes up too much space; carpeted with mats, it awaits an imam and the faithful. Mohammed never thought about whether his children were good or bad Muslims, whether they observed Ramadan, prayed, drank alcohol—no, impossible to imagine. On the contrary, he envisioned them all there and himself up front, leading the prayer, while they submitted dutifully to God's will. He saw them, heard them asking God for help and good fortune—and at that very instant, draped in black from head to toe, a dark silhouette appeared, wearing black gloves and *babouches*, a moving mass, perhaps a woman, or else a thief hiding behind that veil, a shadow circling the house again and again, a strange, heavy, enigmatic presence. Who's there? asked Mohammed. Silence. He felt a cold wind blow by as the shadow swelled up and vanished. Mohammed was afraid, not of being attacked, but of meeting a messenger of misfortune. Like all those of his tribe, he was superstitious, although he would never have admitted it, since only women believe such nonsense.

That *black thing* did not augur well; it could have been a message from the devil, or from some evildoer, a jealous neighbor trying to frighten him or cast a wicked spell. Mohammed knew that envy and hypocrisy thrived in his village, and his wife had even given him talismans to wear against the jealousy of his own family. It's only natural, she'd told him, that when someone manages to climb out of a hole, people do their best to pull him back in. They can't bear it that others enjoy good health and manage to emigrate, because to them emigration is a fantastic stroke of luck, so watch out: your own nephews and cousins see you as the sacrificial lamb of Eid to be shared among themselves when you arrive in that car full of presents. Be careful: it's the people closest to you who are the most envious, and dangerous, for they mean you harm.

Mohammed said prayers, then said them again, but he had an uneasy feeling of foreboding. Although he was physically courageous, this was beyond him. Seized with uncertainty, he felt a painful emptiness burning in the pit of his stomach and wondered if he was having a touch of after-dinner heartburn, but his emotional turmoil grew as he heard the black thing murmuring, grinding its teeth as it came and went.

Mohammed recited the *shahada* several times: *Ach hadou anna la ilaha illa Llah, Mohammed rassoulu Llah*. . . . He watched the phantom flit off, a cloud of dust in its wake. Then he made his ablutions with the water in the bottom of a jar and said a few prayers as if to erase that grim vision, or at least keep it at a distance. When a bat crisscrossing the courtyard brushed by him, he stumbled. Then he fell so deeply asleep that he did not dream at all.

The following evening, after sunset, he climbed up a lopsided ladder to the roof terrace, where he had pitched a tent that in summer would provide a place for sleeping in the cool night air. He thought some more about the thing in black. And again it appeared, this time with part of its face uncovered. It addressed him as if it were a member of his family, and although Mohammed called on God and his prophet, praying for their protection, the thing grew bigger as it spoke to him, now in Berber, now in Arabic.

Pour soul! Meskin! Alas for you! You have spent all your money on this building, to dance on your head, walk on your hands, eat spiny hedgehog, and drink milk full of sand! You will choke and die smothered because no one will come to your aid: you have built a house on the only land that does not belong to humans. You have violated the secret of the masters of this place; you have disturbed them, hurt them, and this house will remain empty, empty, for no soul will ever enter here, and yours is kept outside, because you did not know what you were doing, but from the next night of Destiny onward, you will go hence. You will leave the house to the masters of this place, those who live in the depths of wells and the vaults of the sky, those who burn all that their eyes behold, those who leave no trace and know neither fear nor shame, those who are stronger than Satan because they have always been here, for hundreds and thousands of years, those who love not the imprudent, the foolish, the careless who think to drive them away by reciting a few prayers. Meskin! Alas for you! All that for naught! Gaze not upon me or you will become dust, to be blown by a gust of wind into the distant sands! Listen well to what I tell you, and do as I command! You, men of foreign countries, you have abandoned your lands, and you return to cover them with stones. You are lost and your descendants are lost: they no longer know you; they have already repudiated you; they have escaped from you; and so it has been decreed by the masters of this place, who do not want them, for they are sons of foreign soil, ingrates without roots, without religion. The roots of those shrubs have been cut, burned into cinders and ash. Go to the cemetery to meditate on the tombs of your ancestors, and hearken well to what they will tell you, for they are just and wise: they will say that this house is a mistake, and that one does not live in a mistake—especially when it is immense. One does not come to disturb the masters of this place, because they are invisible: you do not see them but they— they watch and pursue you! To be quit of them, you have only one solution: leave and abandon this house to them, which they will make a place of penitence for those, like you, who have gone astray, those from foreign lands who no longer know who they are or where they came from. One last counsel: do not bother summoning the white-robed men who endlessly chant beautiful words when they think only of the feast to follow.

The shadow disappeared. Mohammed was trembling, bone tired. What should he do? Believe the specter or laugh at it? He made his ablutions and prayed again for God's help and support. Feeling almost at peace, he went off to his old house to sleep. His night was long and painful, cruelly upset by insomnia. Unable to lie still, he would get up, walk around, then collapse back in a bed that creaked and moved as if shaken by invisible hands. He felt that everything was slipping from his grasp, that he had nothing to hold on to. When his Koran fell from the table where it sat covered by material from the paternal shroud, a few pages fluttered loose and were carried away in the air. In a panic, Mohammed would have liked to know which sura had flown away, he would have liked to read it over and over, but that was impossible. He prayed until the sun rose. He tried to find where the missing pages had landed, but there was no trace of them, and when he opened the Koran, he was stunned to see that every page was blank. The verses had been wiped away, swallowed by something unseen. Wrapping the Koran in its piece of shroud, he clutched it to his breast, and fell asleep like that on the floor, on his little prayer rug, huddled up with an expression of agony on his face. Now and then he awoke shivering. It was midsummer, and he was cold, sweating; he could feel a fever rising.

The house mirrored the confusion of his thoughts and in particular the illusions he still harbored. The bathrooms were on the first floor, with Turkish toilets, as in hammams. His children would never use them. They had never seen toilets without a commode, not even in a movie. Mohammed climbed up to the terrace and studied the horizon. Blue, mauve, orange, white: he saw the sky—or imagined it—in his favorite colors. The air was pure, without the slightest breath of wind. A great silence enveloped this world, his world. Gradually he began to feel better there, as if reconciled with himself and this outside world; he had settled in there and no longer heard the distant sounds of the road or the words of the black-clothed shadow. Looking around, he could see that he was the only man to possess such a big house, and that didn't worry him at all. On the contrary, he felt proud: he, at least, had thought of his family, unlike those immigrants who abandoned wife and children and came home to work in their fields while waiting to marry a little shepherdess.

Mohammed went from floor to floor, counting the rooms, losing track and starting over. He spent the evening floundering in calculations, trying in vain to find out how much all this had cost him. At bedtime, he realized there was no water to perform his ablutions before the last prayer of the day. He went to his old house, washed quickly, and returned to the new house, determined to get it ready for his long-cherished goal, his dream, his passion: to welcome his children as the real head of a family, like a lord, a responsible father. He reflected that other men have the drive and aspiration to amass a fortune, or to become a government minister or a stationmaster, whereas his ambition was of the utmost simplicity: to gather his children around him. That was not too much to ask of God, of LaFrance, of the vicissitudes of life—to bring his children here, to this dry countryside, and that unparalleled house, at his age, in this year when his life had changed rhythm and direction.

He considered each of his children in turn. Mourad, the eldest: he's kind, obedient, and eager for my blessing; he'll come, even though he's married to a Christian. Rachid, who calls himself Richard, is uncomfortable in his own skin; he got away from me early on, spending more time playing in our building's courtyard than doing his homework. But he'll come if his big brother insists. Othmane is a good boy; he'll do what his wife tells him, though. A Moroccan woman from Casablanca, she has never liked us and thinks herself better than all of us put together, simply because her parents weren't emigrants, so I'm not sure they'll come. Jamila will, however, because it would provide a chance for our reconciliation, yet I'm doubtful about her as well because she holds a grudge and is as stubborn as I am. As for Nabile, he'll be so happy to be here, with me. And my last little girl, Rekya, she'll obey me without question. At least I think so.

One Friday evening, ignoring the threats of the black thing, Mohammed summoned the readers of the Koran. Among them he noticed a very tall, slender man all in white, to whom he mentioned the black shadow, which made the other man smile. During the reading, a butcher cut the throat of a calf on the threshold while Mohammed's wife burned incense within the house and poured a few drops of milk in all the corners. The house was blessed but uninhabitable. Prayers recited in a droning voice echoed within the walls in a strange, disturbing way, and when a few thin fissures appeared on those walls, one reader rose and ran off, convinced that jinns were at work.*

Out on the patio, the men ate in silence (and rather quickly) from a large platter of couscous. The tall man took Mohammed aside to tell him confidentially that his house needed more protection, that a single evening of reading would not be enough. The demon's resistance must be overcome, he told him.

I believe that the people of the house, the owners, the ones you have disturbed, are demanding reparation, and only the word of God is effective against these beings who emerge from the stones in a black dust that swells into a menacing presence. You must double the number of readers, even if you have to bring them in from Bouya Omar—you know, the saint who cures madmen: they will know how to address the wicked creatures that swarm under the earth, waiting to find you alone and tear you to pieces.* Do you remember what happened some ten years ago, when Bouchta defied them? No, you don't remember, or you weren't there; well, the poor man fell into a hole that quickly filled up with dirt—and he was gone! And yet he'd been warned, told that the property, bought for a mouthful of bread, was inhabited by the invisible people—you know who I mean—but he wouldn't listen to anyone, didn't want to know. One evening, even before he'd begun to build, while he was out walking around the property, the earth just swallowed him up without a trace, so he never even had a proper funeral, since the body had vanished. It's a serious matter; perhaps you think I'm merely telling stories, but the facts are there. In any case, as a good Muslim you have nothing to fear. Don't forget: next Friday, an entire night of reading.

After everyone was gone, Mohammed and his wife found themselves staring at a headless calf soaked in blood. All they could do was stand there. They looked at each other, then left the house in the middle of a moonless night filled with clouds in the shape of calves' heads. Early the next morning the butcher took the animal away to cut it up. Each family received its share of meat. The portions were fair, so the villagers' comments were more or less polite.

16

With the last of his savings, Mohammed bought furnishings for part of the house, including a sprung leather armchair he delivered to a spot outside his front door in a rented Honda. Taking advantage of the long shopping trip to Marrakech, he'd phoned all his children to invite them to join him and had even forced himself to call Jamila, whom he had expelled from his life when she'd married a European. He'd had to leave messages on everyone else's answering machines; Jamila had been the only one home.

It's your father, yes I'm fine, in fact, things are going very well: the house is finished and I'm expecting you, so come, my daughter, you'll see how big and beautiful it is, the loveliest house in the whole village. . . . What do you mean you can't? You're saying no to your father, who spent months building a little palace for you? No, my daughter, you'll come for Eid al-

Kebir. Arrange things with your brothers and come as a group: drive carefully, no speeding, I bless you, my daughter, may God keep you and give you health and happiness, see you soon, my daughter. As he was about to hang up, he heard her shout, But, Papa, are you crazy? What's this business about a house? Do you think I can just leave work, abandon my husband, and come prance around out in the sticks in your dinky little dump? Papa, please, wake up! The world has changed, and I'm not the little girl you used to shower with candies anymore. That's *over*—give up, move on, forget this house and this idea of bring-ing us all back together as if we didn't have our own lives to live. . . . Come on, Papa, don't wear yourself out. Bye-bye, hugs and kisses. . . .

Mohammed was somewhat shaken, and perplexed, but he trusted his intuition: she would come.

For all the others, he left a message, which he had always refused to do when he was in France: The house is ready, it's big, you each have your room—come, I'm expecting you so we can celebrate Eid al-Kebir together: I've bought six sheep, so you'll each have your own. You'll see how handsome and spa-cious the house is, full of light and sweet smells. May God keep you! I'm looking forward to seeing you! If you drive down, be careful! The whole village is expecting you! We'll finally be able to live as one big happy family! He dialed Jamila again, leaving a message when she didn't pick up, speaking, perhaps, into a void: Jamila, my daughter, it's your father calling you. I didn't understand what you just told me. I'm waiting for you in the house, in the village, for the feast of Eid al-Kebir. It's a family reunion, so come without your husband! I'm counting on you!

I spoke to their machines, Mohammed told his wife. I hope those things will transmit my messages without changing them—unless they add that children should obey their father!

Mohammed was absolutely certain: his family reunion would indeed take place. He would finally have his happy ending.

The evening before the festival, he asked one of his nephews, the deaf-mute shepherd, to wait at the entrance to the village for the arriving visitors, to show them the rest of the way. Meanwhile Mohammed sat in his armchair, in the shade near the front door of the house, and waited. He fiddled with some prayer beads, trying to be patient, and gradually grew calmer, although he still felt twinges of anxiety. His wife had already gone to bed back in their old house, and Mohammed felt a little lonely, not abandoned, exactly, but rather misunderstood. Why isn't she here, by my side? Why would she rather sleep, when the children will soon be arriving? She must be tired, she must have her reasons. Perhaps she'll be overjoyed tomorrow to see all of them reunited with us in this beautiful house, and she'll thank me. It's not our custom to say thank you, but we show our satisfaction with a gesture or a smile.

Strange . . . I don't remember ever laughing with my wife. No great peals of mirth like some people have, no familiarity. We don't talk much. I can't remember ever having any long discussions with her, either. I think we agree about everything. We've never had an argument. That's normal—we're married. That's what marriage is: the wife agrees with her husband. That's how it is with us anyway. But now, tonight, I don't understand why she isn't with me. Doesn't she like the house? She hasn't said anything to me. I guess she thinks it's too big. Maybe she's right, but a family house should be large. I know it doesn't look like any other house in the village. My wife fears the evil eye, and this house can be seen from all sides. She must be tired, or else she's praying to God to guide our children here. I know her; she's not trying to be mean to me; she's just busy making sure our plan succeeds: burning incense, pouring milk in the corners of each room, hanging a talisman on the sole tree in the village, circling a slaughtered rooster seven times, hiring a few benevolent sorcerers to protect us from bad luck, envy, jealousy, problems created by our enemies.

I can't think of any enemies; I don't have any. It's shadows that pass by and leave their foul odor behind—I've never done a thing to make enemies. I'm so modest, so simple, that others don't bother envying me, I'm too small for jealousy to notice. My wife believes otherwise, she has always practiced those rituals and they don't bother me. It's best to be careful—you never know. The evil eye! Even the Prophet, it seems, knew about that. Can an eye look with hatred or envy at someone and bring him down? It's impossible, yet . . . I do believe in it, but I don't want to believe in it too much. One day a fellow at the mosque looked at me hard and said, You, they're after you. I turned around but there was no one there, and he laughed at me. No, it's an eye that's after you, a big evil eye. It's obvious, someone's jealous and wants to hurt you, so here, take these plant leaves, put them in a teapot, and drink their essence; it will drive away the evil eye. If you want, come see me. I've even got an herb that fights fear, yes, it's true, and for once it's foreigners that made the discovery—in Italy, I heard.

No one came. No sound of a car engine, no cloud of dust, nothing. The silence was unnatural. No birds or insects flew by. Nothing moved. Everything froze in place. It was as if the whole world had gone quiet. The silence inside Mohammed was engulfing that of the world. He was there, his heart full of questions and expectation, with only one prayer, murmured like a last wish. Leaning to one side, the house cast a shadow that made it even more imposing, almost threatening. In the bright sky, the twinkling stars left Mohammed feeling rather dizzy, as if he were on a voyage, suspended between heaven and earth, and gazing up at them he thought he saw people, roads, streaks of white. He stared at the moon but could not see a single one of his children there. People say you can see loved ones in the moon. Mohammed couldn't find anything familiar. The moon was opaque. He let himself drift off, dozed a little. Impossible to really fall asleep. He was watching, his eye on the horizon; his head felt heavy, and there was sadness in his heart. He couldn't feel his legs anymore but didn't care.

Waiting was a painful ordeal, yet not without hope. Mohammed had rarely waited for anyone, and he remembered how he'd haunted the corridors of Moroccan and French government buildings as well as the halls of the hospital where his wife had given birth. He hadn't paced up and down but found a bench and stayed there. Once a nurse had asked him if he wanted to see his child being born. No, madame, that's just not done!

There he was, and for a few seconds he forgot what he was doing. His goodness was that of a man who does not know how to lie. Even for a joke, to make his children laugh, Mohammed had never lied. He was good and paid no mind to what others said. A kind man, with a single weakness written all over his face. One of his daughters had once told him, It's so obvious that you're a pushover! It was just a remark, not an insult; a child would not disrespect her father, it's not done. Mohammed had wondered why children these days would consider kindness a sign of weakness. Did one have to be hard, authoritarian, and unjust to be strong, respected, admired?

Waiting for the night to end, as if all would become simple in the morning. Waiting for dawn, the sky's pallor and fatigue, and the resolution to begin the first prayer of the day. Waiting for one's eyes to close on the light at last for the last time. Waiting, and saying nothing. Not protesting or growing impatient, withdrawing into the silence, into that expectation whose end he could not see. Getting through the night the way one gets through a police barricade or an ordeal. Going to the end of the night, crossing frozen lakes, climbing mountains, passing from one tree to another, steering clear of the big rocks, the wild animals, the wicked people, avoiding interrogations, and above all, not feeling any regret or exhaustion. Making the night a friend, a companion, steeping oneself in its dust and its lassitude.

The woman was white, wrapped in a white veil. Approaching Mohammed, she held out her right hand, signaling him to follow her, and wide-eyed, he went along with this strange invitation. The woman was light on her feet, walking on tiptoe like a dancer; she took one of Mohammed's thick, callused hands in her cold grasp and drew him after her as if afraid of losing him along the way. He followed her, smiling, and perhaps even happy. He had become light too. He knew all this was a dream and prayed, If only it doesn't stop, and then he felt ashamed. In fact, it was a dream within a different dream. He had been thinking about an angel who would bring his children back to him. Mohammed and his guide soon found themselves in what appeared to be a deserted oasis, where everything was blue: sky, earth, water, palm trees, fruit, carpets. He looked at the woman, studying this face that seemed vaguely familiar, for she had the grace and lithe elegance of his wife when they first married. He also saw a resemblance to one of his daughters, but when he went closer to the woman, everything changed, and her face became one that he had never seen before. Gently, she took off his clothes, invited him to enter a bathtub, washed him, scrubbed his back, added rose water to the bath, and while drying him stroked his shoulders, arms, and hands, which she delicately kissed. After handing him a white linen djellaba, she led him to a large sofa, where she sat down beside him and fed him fruit. After drinking some almond milk, Mohammed fell serenely asleep, gently caressed by the beautiful stranger. The dream within the dream drifted away with the night.

17

Mohammed was awakened in the morning by the sobbing of the shepherd, who must have been thinking that none of us has the right to forsake our parents, to refuse their invitation. In his grief the deaf-mute saw France as a devourer of children and decided that all in all, he was fortunate never to have left the country. He was weeping alone, leaning on Mohammed's shoulder, and as he wept, he sensed that Mohammed would soon succumb to sorrow. The shepherd looked at the house, which seemed to him like a mountain, a heap of useless stones. He had never seen so grand a dwelling, not even in the city. Marveling that it was as big as Mohammed's heart, he left, wiping away his tears.

Mohammed, however, did not move, despite the appeals of his wife, who had rejoined him. He was there, sitting in the old leather armchair bought at the flea market in Marrakech, immobile, eternal, in front of an immense, empty house, surrounded by a desert landscape swept by a cunning wind, immersed in a heavy silence. Late that evening, his wife tried to convince him to come home with her to their old house, but he wouldn't budge: Mohammed had not given up hope of seeing his children arrive, even in the dark of night. His wife draped over his shoulders a woolen blanket woven by the village women and left a loaf of bread, some olives, and a bottle of water by his chair. Mohammed said nothing; his expression was fixed, his features drawn, his mood unfathomable. His wife thought he would grow tired and come home to the old house in the end.

The air was cool, the night mild, and there was no one on the main road. Mohammed dozed off. He dreamed he saw the black shadow holding the hand of the white shadow—the shadow of the tall and slender reader of the Koran—as the two were dancing around a tomb, and the tomb was his. He saw himself in that hole, buried while he was still breathing: he struggled, trying to free himself from the shroud, but in vain. Earth was tossed onto his face, then great stones that were bound together with concrete. It all happened very quickly. Silence; then his heart stopped.

Mohammed started awake and drank a swallow of water. The night was vast. Dark, and deep. He would have liked to stand up to go pee, but something or someone was holding him back. He didn't feel like calling for his wife. So he pissed in his pants. Mortified, he tried again to rise but felt nailed to that accursed armchair, which had once belonged to an old French colonial family. A few springs had pierced the leather and were hurting him. His movements were sluggish, his limbs heavy; his respiration grew slow and halting. He felt the weight of the stones and concrete on his shoulders, and remembered that it is at such a moment that God sends two angels to gather in the last words of those who are dying. While he waited for these envoys, Mohammed decided to tell them everything, get it all off his chest, and emphasize the fact that something had murdered him, that his death was unnatural, for someone had pushed him into this hole, kicking him and mocking both him and his house. But the angels did not come.

Mohammed was crushed. Why should he be the only Muslim to be denied the visit of the angels? Unless it was a sign that all this meant nothing, that he'd been tricked, made a fool of. His rigid arms would no longer move. His head, same thing. Again he felt the hot flow of urine along his legs. He could no longer stop peeing; it was like a fountain of lukewarm water, and he wasn't even ashamed anymore. What point was there in rising to clean himself up, shave, dab on some scent, and clothe himself in white? No one would come. No one would ever remember him.

An abandoned man will begin to smell bad. Mohammed stank, and not just from the night's urine: he stank everywhere, like rancid butter. His entire body weighed him down, but he finally managed to raise one arm and felt movement return, freeing him from imprisonment in that chair he'd used as a toilet. He called out for his wife, who hurried to help him rise and visit the village barber, then entrusted him to one of his brothers, who went with him to the hammam, where Moham-med washed himself clean of that horrible night, one of those nights to laugh about with the man who will dig your grave. Alone in the dim light, the two men sat without speaking, and Mohammed scrubbed hard at his skin to rid himself of that episode, which had left the taste of ashes in his mouth. When he thought he glimpsed the black shadow passing by, he sought reassurance by calling on God. If I were in France, he thought, I would be in a hospital, where doctors and specialists would confer over my case and give me medicine to help me sleep without nightmares. Perhaps they would even summon my family to my bedside. LaFrance is a wonderful country because it takes good care of its sick. Here you're better off never setting foot in a hospital; I'm telling you for your own good! Better the hammam than the hospital.

Mohammed left the hammam a new man. No longer impa-tient or anxious, he made peace with time, giving it free rein, but most of all he kept faith with his obsession. He spent the day at the mosque, renewing old ties with people who had never left the village and thought the world stopped at the end of their dirt road. They prayed like robots, babbling things only God could understand. Mohammed wasn't surprised and reflected that he too might have wound up like them.

That evening he took up his place in the colonial armchair, which his wife had been careful to clean, and despite the irritating springs he found it comfortable. His wife brought him food and a small transistor on which he could listen to music, but the radio station played the raucous favorites of young people, so he turned it off. He remembered the flute he'd played as a boy tending sheep, and smiled. Those days were long gone. And yet he thought he heard a flute playing somewhere on the other side of the hill. He had given his deaf-mute cousin some money to go buy a pair of binoculars from the man who'd sold him the armchair, and now he settled himself into that chair, placed the binoculars on his lap, and, eager to use them, awaited the slightest noise or movement, even though he couldn't see a thing in the darkness. He closed his eyes and rested his hands on the binoculars, reassured by their presence.

The moon was full, and he slept fitfully. He had a dream he'd had several times before and knew quite well: standing alone and unable to move in the middle of a vast, white space, he catches sight in the distance of shadows that advance toward him without ever reaching him. The weight of a dead donkey on his back traps him in his furious immobility, and this burden on his body, this impression of being hamstrung by an outside force, frightens him to the core. Trying to call for help, Mohammed cannot make a sound. This bad dream is called the "night donkey." And donkeys are such gentle animals during the day! he thought. Mohammed had lost all memory of the white woman and her oasis. To reach it again, he would have had to cross a dream that opens onto another dream, but his imagination was weakening, and his dreams were turning into simplified sketches of what he was hoping and waiting for, night and day.

At sunrise, when Mohammed tried to get to his feet for the dawn prayer, he again found himself paralyzed, but he quickly ceased struggling and prayed with his eyes, as if he'd been prostrate in bed with a grave illness. I'm sick, yes, but with what? This malady has no name, striking without warning and from all sides. No one here can diagnose it. If I had the strength—and above all, if I hadn't summoned my children here—I would willingly have gone to the Piti, the Pitié-Salpêtrière hospital right next to the Austerlitz railroad station in Paris; yes, I'm sure they would know what I have, but, well . . . I can't miss my children's arrival; they must be on the way. They're the ones coming toward me in the night donkey dream: I see them, I think I even hear them, but they never arrive. It's strange. They must be held up at the border by one of those corrupt customs officials, who's probably suggesting things they don't understand. How could anyone expect my children to know that *dwar maána*, "turn our way," means "grease my palm"! They're not familiar with those expressions I've heard so many times in my life. A small bribe or two, and they would already be here. But my children were not brought up around such petty schemes.

When the first rays of the sun fell upon him, Mohammed realized that he smelled bad again, and thought, How much a man stinks when he's left on his own! An invisible wound, difficult to track down, was tormenting him. Even though he hadn't eaten anything, the pain he felt was not around his stomach but in his liver. As he stared at the horizon, his vision became blurred. It was only when Mohammed tried to shift his position slightly that he noticed how the armchair was slowly sinking into the earth. Untouched by human hands, the old chair had rooted itself into the ground like a solidly anchored stake. Like an old boat cast up on a deserted beach, like some now useless piece of junk. Each day, the armchair was slowly sinking a little more. Its leather had greatly aged, and through new gashes, the springs now appeared as keen blades that cut him when he moved. Drops of his blood mingled with his urine and tears. Mohammed wept like a child and could not stop. At her wit's end, his wife left for Marrakech to phone their children.

18

The odor Mohammed gave off was suffocating. Was he refusing to leave his armchair or was something—or someone—holding him back? The fat flies buzzing around him made an unnerving noise, some of them zeroing in on him as if he were a butchered carcass. Even though wasps had joined the attack, Mohammed would not budge.

Everyone in his tribe filed past, begging him to relent, to leave that accursed armchair, wash himself, and wait for his children at home. Stubborn and determined, Mohammed would neither eat nor speak. Starving cats, lost dogs, and a jackal were circling the house, and some beggars from another village even arrived to prowl around. Black birds of prey hovered overhead. Taking fright, the villagers went away, calling upon God for mercy and deliverance. The wisest man among them lingered to recite the six verses of the last sura, "Mankind": "Say: I seek refuge in the Lord of mankind, the King of mankind, the God of mankind, so that he may deliver me from the seductions of Satan, who breathes evil into the human heart. May he defend me against the working of jinns and men." The man returned later to recite the last verses of the ninth sura, "Repentance": "Now has come unto you a distinguished messenger. It grieves him that you should suffer; he watches zealously over you, and to believers he is most kind and merciful. But if they turn him away, let him say, 'Allah suffices me: there is no god but he. In him is my trust, and he is lord and master of the sublime throne.'"

These prayers soothed Mohammed: his face grew serene as lines of pain and worry vanished one by one. It was perhaps then that he plumbed the depths of his soul, a descent that allowed him to rise and to embrace absolute peace.

A cousin managed to gather the tribe together to pray for the soul of Mohammed, a man mistreated by exile and France: Mohammed is a lost man, a suffering man, for France has taken his children from him; France gave him work, and then took everything he had. This we say for all those who dream of seeking work abroad: over there our values are worth nothing; over there our language is worth nothing; over there our traditions are not respected. Look at poor Mohammed! He was a wise man, a good Muslim, and here he is today, abandoned, miserable, at the edge of a madness that has already begun to claim him. We will say a few prayers so that God will come to his rescue: we will begin the prayer for deliverance.

Although he could hear the sound of the chanting, Mohammed was already far away, far from the house, the village, and the world. His wife, who had left for France to try to convince the children to visit him, kept saying to herself, We belong to God; nothing belongs to us; we are God's creatures; we have no choice; he is the one who has chosen our path, and it is to him that we return; we are only passing through.

After thirty days Mohammed was unrecognizable, he had grown so thin. He smelled worse and worse, and no one went near him. The armchair was practically underground, and Mohammed as well: only his head and part of his shoulders were still visible. No human hands had buried the chair, which had sunk of its own accord, slowly, day after day. Mohammed had felt this gradual descent, but done nothing. Perhaps he desired it deeply and was allowing his body to become entangled in the chair springs, letting his weight accelerate the collapse. He was anxious to be done with it, to leave without openly disobeying God, without defying him by taking his own life. As a good Muslim, he would not commit suicide. He let himself progress toward the end, making no effort to free himself and recover his taste for life. But his life was over, its meaning held hostage by the egotism or thoughtlessness of his children. His eyes were closed. He no longer wished to see the spectacle of the world. He had renounced the example of the mystic who abandons the envelope of the body to journey into the soul's heart. He had turned out the lights, closing his eyes and his heart, delivering himself up to his soul, which he had charged with guiding him on toward the sublime silence.

The flies came seeking their nourishment, for Mohammed had set down his life and was no longer waiting for his children but for release, the death he silently demanded from the mercy of heaven. His wife had returned with Nabile; his other children wished neither to believe her nor to leave their work to go comfort a man in the throes of delirium. Crazed with grief, Nabile began to speak clearly, urging the man he considered his father to rise and give him his hand so they could go together to the hammam. Nabile went around and around the chair, of which only the tattered arms could still be seen, waiting for Mohammed to awaken from his long slumber. Nabile washed the dying man's head with a bucket of warm water, but Mohammed was breathing ever more slowly: he was going. Without a word, as a faint smile played about his lips, he drifted into a deep sleep. He asked nothing of the sky or the passing clouds. All became simple, limpid: whatever or whomever he was dying for had fallen down the well of his childhood; he no longer saw them, could no longer distinguish their faces, no longer heard the sound of their voices.

By the fortieth day, the earth had swallowed up his head. Someone cried out, Gone! Mohammed has gone to God! The village has its saint! We have our saint! God has not forgotten us! The house has not been built for nothing; it will be his tomb, his marabout! God is great! God is great! An old woman sitting on a stone spoke up: Wonderful! We haven't any water, we haven't any wheat, we haven't any electricity, but we have a saint! That's just fine! I'm leaving, off to find some water and a scrap of shade. If I ever pray at a marabout, it will be a spring, a pool of water—that's what life is! The others replied, You madwoman, we know you: we've seen you smoking and even drinking fermented grape juice, so you—you've no right to speak, and you had better bow before our saint, who has gone far away to return by the grace of God.

Foul odors no longer seeped from the tomb Mohammed's body had dug for weeks, and people wondered how they could pull him out of that hole to wash his body and wrap it in a shroud. When the grave diggers reached him, they were shocked: Mohammed was enveloped in a white shroud perfumed with incense that smelled like paradise. His body had been perfectly prepared for burial. The grave diggers drew back, shouldered their picks, and left.

There was Mohammed's tomb, before the front door of

the house. The next morning people found it freshly white-washed, and a stele had appeared, inscribed with these words:

IN THE NAME OF GOD THE GRACIOUS AND MERCIFUL:
HERE LIES A MAN, A FAITHFUL BELIEVER;
HIS SUFFERING IS OVER;
MAY THE GRACE AND MERCY OF GOD BE UPON HIM;
WE BELONG TO GOD, AND TO GOD WE SHALL RETURN.

No one ever found out who had constructed this monument. People came from all around to pray, and some of them left offerings at the front door to the big house. The wasps and flies went away, as did the cats and dogs. A heavenly fragrance issued from the grave, which in a few days became thickly carpeted with lush green grass and dotted with wildflowers. A stranger planted a tree he'd brought from afar. Now there was cool shade, and peace. And that was how Mohammed Thimmigrant, the man slain by his retirement, vanished from this earth.

Paris, Tangier
April 2005–July 2008

Notes

1   Islam's most sacred site is a shrine in Mecca, al-Kaaba; Muslims everywhere face it during prayers. One of the Five Pillars of Islam is the hajj, the largest annual pilgrimage in the world, which all Muslims should perform at least once, after which he or she uses the honorific title Hajji or Hajja. One ritual of both the hajj and the *umrah* (a lesser pilgrimage) is the circumambulation of the Kaaba, performed by as many as two million pilgrims at a time. The hajj ends with the celebration of Eid al-Kebir, during which animals are slaughtered to commemorate Abraham's willingness to sacrifice his son at God's command.

11   The Koran contains 114 suras, traditionally arranged in order of decreasing length. Each sura is named for a word or name mentioned in one of its sections.

27   During the European heat wave of 2003, an estimated 11,435 people died in France in August, when much of the population went on vacation. The authorities had no disaster plans for

heat waves, and some officials even denied there was a health crisis until the heat had claimed hundreds of victims, many of them elderly people living alone or left behind at home. Some bodies remained unclaimed for weeks because family members were still on holiday.

51 On October 17, 1961, a year before the end of the Algerian War (1954–62), thirty thousand Algerians demonstrated peacefully in Paris in support of the pro-independence Algerian FLN. Maurice Papon, the Paris police chief (and infamous war criminal), promised his twenty thousand officers protection from prosecution—and demonstrators were shot, clubbed, thrown into the Seine to drown, murdered in the very courtyard of the Préfecture de Police, or simply "disappeared." Only after thirty-seven years of denial did the French government admit responsibility, in 1998, for this atrocity, which claimed an estimated two hundred victims.

57 Jean-Marie Le Pen, founder of the National Front party, is a reactionary who supports sweeping restrictions on immigration. In the first round of voting in the French presidential election of 2002, he unexpectedly beat Lionel Jospin, the main left candidate, which meant that the deeply unpopular Jacques Chirac then ran against the even more unpopular Le Pen as the lesser of two evils, and won. (Sample election slogan: "Vote for the crook, not the fascist.")

61 The Makhzen is the governing elite in Morocco, a feudal institution something like the Russian *nomenklatúra*. This un-

touchable network of important men in finance, the military, the police, and government, as well as tribal leaders and the royal family, revolves around the king, who is still all-powerful in Morocco. The present king's father, Hassan II (reigned 1961–99), adopted a market-based economy (with underwhelming success) and allowed the institution of some mechanisms of parliamentary democracy (which the conservative king essentially ignored). Opposition to Hassan's despotic rule was ruthlessly repressed: many dissidents were exiled, jailed, or killed. In his novel *This Blinding Absence of Light*, Tahar Ben Jelloun describes the secret underground prison, a series of six-by-three-foot cells, in which men unwittingly involved in an attempted coup spent twenty years in utter darkness; the few survivors were freed when the outside world discovered and voiced outrage at such cruelty. King Mohammed VI presents himself as an enlightened ruler battling poverty and corruption, a (modest) champion of women's rights and democracy. His economic reforms have seen some progress, and Morocco's dismal human rights record has improved, but the old problems of repression and abject poverty remain. The king remains a dictator in almost complete command of a country without any real separation of powers or government accountability.

70 "Al-Baqara" ("The Heifer") is the second sura; it sums up the teaching of the Koran and takes its name from a brief reference to Moses, who tells his reluctant people that God com-

mands them to sacrifice a cow. The parable of the heifer illustrates the inadequacy of blind or reluctant obedience, for when true faith is lost, empty compliance means nothing, and the soul begins to die.

78 "Marriage for pleasure" is a Muslim tradition that permits temporary religiously sanctioned sex: a marriage contract is drawn up for a period ranging from an hour to a year, without any commitments or religious ceremony. When the time limit is up, the "marriage" automatically dissolves.

90 Jamaa al-Fna is the vast square at the heart of the old city in Marrakech, an open-air market and arena for festivals, street performers, storytellers, diviners, dancers, musicians, peddlers, and hustlers of all kinds. After dark, dozens of food stalls spring up and the square becomes even more crowded.

91 A *ryad* (Arabic for "garden") is a traditional Moroccan home built around an interior garden and modeled on the Roman villa. Many of these newly fashionable *ryads* have been renovated or converted into restaurants or hotels.

96 The Berbers are the indigenous peoples of Northwestern Africa. Today the largest number of Berbers is in Morocco; the northeastern highlands of Algeria and Tunisia are home to a Berber people called the Kabyles. Some Berbers speak Arabic as well as French in the post-colonial Maghreb, but many speak only Tamazight and often face discrimination. Berbers tend to live in less-developed rural areas and can be considered "backward" by Arabs.

97   Islamic invaders began settling southern Spain in 711, and travelers in Andalusia still marvel at the surviving wonders of their civilization, but by 1238 wars of reconquest waged by Christian rulers had reclaimed almost all of Muslim Spain from *los moros*. In 1492, the Reyes Católicos (Catholic Monarchs) drove the last sultan of Granada into exile, ending Moorish rule in Spain.

114   The *shahada* is the profession of faith: "*Ach hadou anna la ilaha illa Llah, Mohammed rassoulu Llah*" (I affirm that there is no God but Allah and that Mohammed is his prophet). A person may become a Muslim simply by reciting the *shahada*, with sincerity, in front of witnesses.

118   On October 27, 2005, two French boys of North African descent were electrocuted while hiding in an electrical substation from the police. Parisian suburbs heavily populated by Arab and African immigrant families erupted in rioting that spread throughout France, and there were similar incidents in 2006 and 2007. The government initially adopted a law-and-order response to the violence, which it linked to illegal immigration and the separatist practices of Islam, but the rioters were overwhelmingly native-born youths, and their motives were more complex. In the 1950s and '60s, after France's African empire collapsed, many guest workers flooded into the country from her former colonies, settling mainly just outside Paris to work at industrial jobs that have now grown scarce. Crowded into ugly housing projects and urban slums, and at-

tending often second-rate schools, the children and grand-children of these large African and Arab communities must cope with high unemployment and discrimination. Although the original immigrants indeed found a better life in their adopted country (and could usually return home if necessary), their French-born descendants have few ties to the old country, and while many second- and third-generation immigrants have fit successfully into French society, others in this growing minority do not yet feel truly accepted by their own nation.

152   In the West, a jinn is usually thought of as a "genie in a bottle," but in pre-Islamic Arabian mythology and in Islamic culture the Jinn are a race of supernatural creatures lower than angels, capable of assuming human or animal form and influencing mankind for good or evil. Jinns are invisible to humans unless they choose to be seen by them. Although the Jinn live in their own societies like humans (they eat, marry, and while they may live for hundreds of years, they do die), like angels the Jinn have no substance: whole communities can live comfortably on the head of a pin or cozily in a vast desert waste. They like water and tend to live by creeks and in wells and washrooms, cemeteries and old ruins. They are touchy creatures, however, and it is dangerous to intrude on their territory, even by accident.

153   The popular approach to mental and much physical illness in Morocco derives both from the Berber traditions of animism, which attribute magical powers to nature, and from the tenets

of Islam. In Moroccan sorcery, spiritual power both benign and malignant can reside anywhere—a tree, a bird, a glass of tea—as the natural property of the object, or it can be placed there by human agency. It can be unleashed at random (a traveler tripping on a stone) or can target a specific person. It can also attack without physical contact, via jinns or the evil eye, harming a victim through the envy of other people even without their conscious will.

The Sufis brought Islamic mysticism to Morocco in the twelfth century, and their holy men, the marabouts, acted as intercessors between mankind and the spiritual realm. One of them, Bouya (Father) Omar, gained fame in the sixteenth century by interceding with the Jinn for their human victims and arranging compensation for the spirits' grievances (through animal sacrifices, Koranic readings, prayers, offerings at a marabout's grave). Today a holy man's tomb is likewise called a marabout, and there are many of these simple, white-domed structures throughout Morocco. The marabout of Bouya Omar, not far from Marrakech, is particularly popular with people afflicted by mental illness.

AVAILABLE FROM PENGUIN

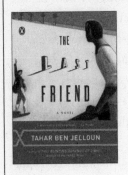  

BY TAHAR BEN JELLOUN

The Last Friend
ISBN 978-0-14-303848-1

Leaving Tangier
ISBN 978-0-14-311465-9

This Blinding Absence of Light
ISBN 978-0-14-303572-5

"Ben Jelloun is arguably Morocco's greatest living author."
—The Guardian

PENGUIN